TOWER OF
THE MEDUSA

TOWER OF THE MEDUSA

LIN CARTER

WILDSIDE PRESS

TOWER OF THE MEDUSA

Published by Wildside Press LLC.
www.wildsidebooks.com

CHAPTER 1

THE DEATH DWARVES

It was on Zha the Jungle Planet that the strange little yellow men with three eyes finally caught up with the Earthman, Kirin.

They came at him in a muddy alleyway behind the Spaceman's Rest. It was a stormy night in the Month of Rains. Lightning flared in storm-dark skies; the nine moons of Zha were veiled behind clouds. Rain lashed the red jungles that hemmed in the little trading port the starmen had built in a raw clearing. It thundered on the sheet-plastic roofs of the equipment huts, the cabins, the store sheds, and turned the narrow, twisting alleys between these buildings into glistening rivers of slick mud.

Out on the landing field, intermittent flares of lightning lit the glossy curving hulls of the merchant ships. The tall vessels loomed up into the stormy heavens like tapering steel projectiles. Wind whistled around them, across the jet-baked duracrete, and shook the walls of the flight control center that climbed on stilt-like metal struts into the rainswept darkness.

Kirin was a tall man, lean and sinewy rather than burly. He had a dark, secretive, mocking face, a sardonic smile and clever, sly black eyes. His hair was a curious dark red inherited from his Celtic father, while his Iberian mother had perhaps contributed the swarthy tone of his skin. He was lithe, supple, swift; nimble as any acrobat. Women found him devilishly attractive. Beneath his ironic mask of mockery they sensed a cold, hard core of bitter loneliness. It posed an irresistible challenge to their femininity:

They would not be women if they did not long to melt that frozen bitterness. As yet, none had succeeded. Kirin had known many women. But he had never known love. Which was just as well, considering the hazardous career which he pursued.

Kirin was a thief.

There were many like him in those dark, troubled days of the Interregnum, between the collapse of the Old Empire and the rise of the New. Man built many forms of society during his first three thousand years in space. The strongest had been the mighty Carina Empire. For six thousand years it had lasted, and its boundaries had included most of the stars in the Carina-Cygnus arm of the galaxy. At last it crumbled from within, and yielded to the attack of the Barbarians from the Rim. In flame and thunder it fell, man's greatest experiment in government. With it passed much of what is called civilization. Trade and communications lapsed; commerce ebbed. World was cut off from world. Technology broke down and science became a jumble of half-forgotten formulas. Cluster by cluster, the star worlds slid into the red murk of barbarism. Magic was reborn, built on the mysterious, micro-miniaturized instruments of the legendary Ancients, whose incredible machines, built to last for eternity, were sensitized to mental controls.

With the rebirth of magic came witchcraft and superstition, and dark nameless cults and evil gods. It seemed, to bitter, disillusioned men like Kirin, that civilization had failed—power lay with the cold, hard, unscrupulous men who had courage or strength or cunning enough to seize it. There were many like him on the Frontier Worlds— outlaws, adventurers, treasure hunters. Men who went boldly forward to take what they wanted.

It was said that things were on the mend. In this one-thousandth year of the Interregnum it was now two centuries since Calastor broke the lingering remnants of the Rim Barbarians and founded the beginnings of the New Empire at Valdamar. For two hundred years the sons of Calastor had been busy. A dozen worlds of the Inner Stars were now leagued together under the banner of the Empire, striving to build civilization anew. From tattered books and aged computers, half-forgotten sciences were being rediscovered. Men built starships again for the first time in a millennium. Commerce between the more settled and peaceful worlds had sprung up; lines of communication were being established. Perhaps the long decline was over, and a new day was dawning. Perhaps.

Kirin put no faith in dreams. He valued only material things he could see and handle. Like jewels.

It was because of jewels that he was stuck here on Zha. He had been after the fabulous Stardrop of Kandahar. There were only seven of them known to man, and six were in the crown of the Valdamar Emperor. The seventh was set in the alabaster brow of an idol on Shuthab in the Dragon Stars. Kirin had been after it when he tripped an invisible alarm-ray and had to flee empty-handed with half the warriors of a dozen worlds howling at his heels. Then the Star Legions of the Empire joined the thief hunt, for Shuthab was allied with Valdamar although not a member world of the Empire. He had to run fast and far to elude pursuit; in fact, he had run all the way to primitive Zha.

Here he had been holed up for the past three months, until the chase and furor died down and the Near Stars would be safe for him to venture into again. With the last of his funds he had purchased a hut and rental space on the landing field for his sleek little speedster. The first month or so had not been so bad. He had gone hunting with the savage Zhayana, trekking through the red jungles on the spoor of dragon cat and flying lions and the other exotic beasts of the Jungle World. The twenty or so other star-men who shared the little trader's encampment with him asked no questions and bothered him little. They were used to mysterious men with shadowy pasts.

But this rude life had long since begun to pall. Kirin was of too active and inquiring a mind, too restless and footloose, to endure this dull existence without boredom. By now he was sick of Zha and everything about it—sick of the little cluster of prefab huts in the raw little clearing hacked by lasers out of the sprawling jungles that covered most of the land surface of Zha—sick of seeing the same hard faces and hearing the same dreary conversation. Even the natives no longer intrigued him, the broad-shouldered, bronze-skinned barbaric warriors with grim eyes and startling manes of metallic crimson who brought priceless dragonskins and mountain crystals and superb native scimitars of ion-steel to trade for power guns and star-man's liquor and energy tools.

And now, on top of it all, the rainy season had come. The perpetual rains that lasted weeks on end had confined him to his cramped little hut on the edge of the clearing and chained him to the companionship of a handful of dull traders and exporters. There was nothing to do but drink and gamble and sleep. Kirin was sick of it all.

But here, at least, he was safe. No pursuit could follow him here. Zha lay far beyond the limits of the New Empire, among the little known and half-explored wilderness worlds of the frontier. Here beyond the border the monitors of Valdamar had no authority, and the fanatic priesthood of Shuthab had no followers. Here he could hide until he was forgotten. All he had to do was keep cool, watch his temper, and endure stolidly the stinking mud, the endless rains, the vile liquor and the dull company. Another month should do it. If I can last another month, he thought.

They were waiting for him in the alley behind the port's only bar, a shed called Spaceman's Rest. There were four of them and they came at him without a word, lunging through the roiling mists, eyes glittering like snakes.

They almost had him in that first half-second, for he was dull-witted from an evening spent hunched over a rear table nursing a bottle of that fiery purple brandy the Eophim distill from the wine-apples of Valthomé. When he reached his limit he paid his bill, drew the hooded weather cloak about his broad shoulders, snapped on the rain-repelling power field, and stepped out into the oily muck of the street, shoulders hunched against the cold drizzle. His mind was lax and befuddled and the last thing in the universe he expected was to be attacked.

But Kirin the thief had not survived this long on the rough Frontier Worlds without developing hair-trigger senses. As the four shadowy figures lunged at him through the fog, he sprang back with a grunt of surprise and tossed back a fold of his cloak to clear his gun hand. The little power gun appeared out of nowhere, so swiftly did he draw. They paid it no attention.

Strange little men they were, surely no monitors from Valdamar, and as unlike the scaly-skinned Reptile Men of Shuthab as could be. They were short, scarcely more than four feet tall, built squat and bowlegged, with sallow yellow skins and three black eyes set triangle-wise in their little ugly faces. They snarled and spat at him as they struck.

He fired. A spear of blinding radiance caught one full in the chest and sent him reeling away to thud against a wall and slide down into the mud, blackened and tattered and reeking of cooked meat. Then his beam accounted for a second of the dwarfed assassins. Its head vanished in a flare of light with a sound such as a giant might make if he clapped his huge hands once.

Then they were at him like snarling hounds worrying a tiger. They were not armed with energy weapons nor with swords, but carried curious little rods of ebony or some smooth slick black wood about eighteen inches long, knobbed at both ends.

They were very adept at the use of these strange weapons.

One laid his rod along Kirin's wrist with a flickering stroke like that of a striking serpent. The blow seemed only to graze his skin but the shock of the blow numbed him from wrist to shoulder. His power gun fell spinning from fingers suddenly strengthless. It clattered and clanged against muddy cobbles and he was unarmed.

But not entirely helpless. He was a tall man, lean and hard. He had long sinewy arms and tough scarred fists, and he knew how to use them. He had fought for his life many times in his far-ranging career of crime, and he knew every trick of in-fighting ever invented by human ingenuity—especially the dirty ones. He kneed one snarling little dwarf in the gut and knocked the other aside with a shrewd blow of the flat of his hand against the side of the throat. The dwarf's neck broke with an audible snap, like a rotten branch underfoot, and the snarling thing slid down in the muck.

Two were dead and two were down, and Kirin stood there in the rain panting, feeling tingles run through his paralyzed arm. It hung there at his side like dead meat and he wondered if it were broken. He bent to snatch up the power gun that had fallen from his benumbed hand. He bent just in time to avoid being brained by one of the knobbed ebony rods. As it was it slammed against his temple with stunning force, it sent red flares of bright agony lancing through his brain. He staggered, almost fell, lurched to his feet and looked around.

There were more of them coming down the alley. Nine of them!

He ran, and that was the first mistake. He should have ducked back in the bar, but there was no time to think. He just let instinct take over, and ran for his life. Boots thudding through the slop underfoot, gasping for breath, he pelted down the misty street to an intersection. He paused and took a swift, all-encompassing glance around. His dire forebodings proved true. They were coming at him from three directions now, and there were about two dozen of them. They came loping through the seething fog like hunting-hounds, silent and deadly, the knobbed batons glistening in their fists.

He turned and ran down the street. The little grading port was not very large, a score of huts at the most. At this time of the month it was largely deserted—a few men were snoring in their cabins, but most of the others were back in the Spaceman's Rest, boozing it up. If he were to yell his lungs out they could not hear, not with the cold rain sleeting down, drumming on the roofs, and the bellowing rumble of thunder.

He was alone, and, in a few minutes, he discovered he was trapped.

So he turned and fought. He snapped up a length of fallen pipe from a tarpaulin-covered pile near a supply shed. He set his broad back up against the rear wall of a large store shed and fought them with everything he had. The long pipe was heavy. Dull steel glistened wetly down its length. It made a terrible weapon. With every blow it killed or maimed. In no time at all, it seemed, seven or eight twisted little corpses lay in the rain, crimsoning the mud.

The dwarfed assassins drew back from the swing of the terrible steel weapon that now glittered wetly red for half its length. He stood against the wall and let the red haze drain from before his eyes and tried to discover the secret of breathing again. One of the deadly knobbed rods had taken him in the solar plexus and his lungs were on fire with the lust for air.

He knew it was only a matter of time. He was far away from the cabins now. There was nothing on these streets but locked sheds and the landing field that lay beyond. He could see the hulls of the ships towering into the murky sky. His own little cruiser was among them. If he could reach it, he would have an impregnable fortress to protect him, for the little flying sticks could not get through a thirteen-inch hull-plate of ion-bathed steel. If...

Out of the fog a knobbed ebony rod flew. He jerked his head aside but a little too late. It smacked the side of his jaw with stunning force. The blow snapped his head back and made stars dance before his eyes. He fell, and the steel pipe rang against the cobbles and rolled out of reach.

Then they came at him again, silent and deadly as panthers. His boot-heel caught one full in the belly. The little monster fell backwards in the slop, gagging and spitting. Three more sprang at his throat. One he slew with a swift jabbing blow to the nerve-clump just below the base of the skull behind the ear—a stroke with stiffened fingers he had learned years ago from a Ghadorian nerve killer he met on Shimar in the Dragon Stars.

But more came at him through the mists. He fought them with everything he had. Never had he battled so desperately, not even that time the murderous priests of Zodah trapped him in the act of stealing the tiara of their harlot queen. But the little men with three eyes were the most deadly adversaries he had ever faced. They fought in utter silence with a grace and skill and economy of strength that was astonishing.

Then he knew them for what they were—trained killers! Members of the weird assassin cult of Pelizon across the cluster from Zha.

The Death Dwarves!

* * * *

Then, somehow, he was out in the open again. He had fought his way through them and the street lay open before him. He ran again, knee-high boots slipping on muddy cobbles, for the space field, and the safety of his ship.

And he almost made it.

A knobbed rod caught him in the back of the skull with staggering force and he went down on his face in the mud. This time he knew he could not rise in time, to turn and face them again. This was the end. Oddly, the thing that nagged at him was not the fact of death, but a question—why? Why were the little men from Pelizon after him? He had never been on Pelizon in his life, or near it for that matter. And even the fanatics of Shuthab, raving for his blood, could not purchase the service of the Death Dwarves. They fought only for their dark gods. They killed only the foes of those gods. Why, then, kill him?

They were almost on him when a shadowy figure loomed out of the mist to confront them. One yellow claw-like hand was at his throat when the mysterious figure stepped forward and intervened. Even as the little dwarf bent over the fallen Kirin, three black eyes glinting with malignant fires, the deadly rod poised for the death-stroke, a slender ivory wand came flickering through the driving rain to brush gently against the dwarf's supple wrist.

It was a light, glancing blow. But it was enough. Suddenly the dwarf sucked in his breath like a hissing serpent and snatched back a hand. Kirin could see the agony in the three eyes. Scalding agony, as if the hand had suddenly been dipped full to the wrist in a beaker of molten lead.

The others fell back before that dancing ivory wand. For a long moment the stranger held them at bay while he reached down, puffing with exertion, and hauled the exhausted, groggy Earthman to his feet.

"That way—my ship," Kirin panted. They backed up, the stranger half-dragging and half-supporting Kirin as his stumbling legs sagged under his weight.

The dwarves came forward through the mist in an ominous ring, circling them and the ship.

Kirin yelled the recognition code and the airlock swung open. He lurched into it.

"Come on," he grunted.

Then a hail of flying rods hurtled into them. Thudding blows that caught them and pummeled them mercilessly. The stranger went sprawling on the slick wet tarmac of the field, out cold with an ugly red bruise above one eye.

Afterwards, Kirin never quite remembered how he managed to drag his unknown rescuer in after him and seal the doors. Things were dark and confused for quite some time thereafter. Then they got darker. In fact, he was out cold.

CHAPTER 2

DOCTOR TEMUJIN

He woke to glowing lights and a thrumming vibration. He and the other man lay in the lock bay but the lock was sealed and they were safe. He lay there groggily, listening for the thud of knobbed blows against the hull, but he heard only the drone of the drive.

"All right, what the hell have you done?" he asked of empty air. A mechanical voice answered from the wall voder.

"Since you were obviously under attack and were in no condition to issue orders personally, Prime Directive alpha-1 went into effect," the ship replied in pleasant, even tones. "I am instructed to protect you and myself on my own initiative, under such circumstances—"

"I know all that," Kirin growled, lurching unsteadily to his feet. "What did you do?"

"I sealed up and lifted off planet into a stable orbit two miles aloft," the ship answered. "You and your companion are in need of medical attention; the cabinet is to your—"

"I know where it is," Kirin grunted, heading for it. "Mix drinks. Use your own initiative."

While the ship busied itself with that delicate task, Kirin activated the robot medical system and dragged his still-nameless rescuer out of the bay to a more comfortable position within reach of the cabinet. While extensible metal instruments probed cuts, swabbed wounds and treated bruises, he took a good long look at the stranger and was puzzled not to recognize him.

He was short and fat and bald as an egg, with tufted brows and an enormous set of bandit-mustachios that gave his fat-jowled red face a piratical look even in repose. It was hard to tell how old he was but old enough, surely, to be Kirin's father, except that he wasn't Kirin's father.

The cabinet gave him a whiff of stimulant that woke him up and Kirin saw that he had mild twinkling blue eyes. And when he opened his mouth, wincing at the assorted cuts and bruises that adorned his physiognomy—to say nothing of the hefty lump above his left eye—Kirin was amused to discover the fellow had an admirable command of invective.

A glastic panel snapped up in the wall, exposing two tumblers of an amber fluid. Ice cubes tinkled enticingly therein as a pressor beam wafted the two containers within reach.

"Lacking specific directives, but cognizant of your tastes in alcoholic beverages, I took the liberty of mixing—" the ship began.

"Dry up!" Kirin snapped. Then as the stranger ogled him, he grinned. "Not you—my loudmouth robot ship. Here, wrap yourself around a little of this." He handed the other a tumbler and watched as the level of the amber fluid descended swiftly.

"Ah!" his companion remarked after a bit. "Although forbidden by my vows, save for medicinal purposes, that hit the spot!" A more comfortable expression settled over the fat red face and the blue eyes twinkled jovially.

"If this mechanical Aesculapius is quite finished ministering to my bodily needs, I might remark that your yonder pneumo looks a mite more comfortable than this deck . . ." said the stranger tentatively. Kirin helped the fat little man to his feet and guided him to one of the two pneumatic chairs in the cabin before the curved control console where lights twinkled softly. The little man settled back with a sigh, shrugging out of his weather cloak. Which reminded Kirin he was still wearing his own. In fact, the repellor field was still on and laboring valiantly to repel air-born moisture, of which there was none. He snapped the field off and tossed the cloak aside: the ship would hang it up.

"Excellent, excellent!" the little man puffed, nodding about. Kirin was unsure as to whether the remark concerned the ship or the drink. Then the other settled the question by remarking, "For a thief, friend Kirin, you travel in style and comfort. Yes, indeed!"

Kirin was suddenly cold and alert. If the fat, smiling little man noticed the sudden chill in the atmosphere he did not show it.

"You seem to have the advantage of me, sir," Kirin said. He lounged in the pneumatic chair, his hand a hair's-breadth from a hidden energy gun clipped under the console.

"Of course, how stupid of me! Temujin, Doctor Temujin," the fat man huffed and wheezed, making a sketchy little bow which looked absurd when performed from a sitting position. "I wonder if this admirable mechanism of yours could possibly—ah—?" he hinted, tapping his empty tumbler suggestively, tufted brows elevated inquiringly.

"Sure. Ship! Two more of the same."

Doctor Temujin fixed him with a shrewd, twinkling little eye.

"You will be wondering how I know you, sir."

"Something of that nature had crossed my mind," Kirin admitted. "Together with a few other questions…" Temujin nodded, accepting another drink.

"Those ugly little monsters were Death Dwarves from Pelizon," the little man puffed. He dipped into the tumbler and drank thirstily. When he came up for air, he said, "They came to Zha to slay you; I came to save your life. Alas, I was almost too late for the appointment… and I believe, sir, you ended up by saving mine."

Kirin's cold eyes narrowed thoughtfully. "Since I have never had occasion to visit Pelizon, I fail to understand how I have earned the enmity of the Death Dwarves," he said slowly. "And for that matter, I am a bit puzzled as to how you knew of my danger or why you concerned yourself with it."

The other drained the tumbler and set it down with a little grunt of satisfaction. He settled back in his pneumatic chair, folded his hands comfortably over his fat middle, and beamed at Kirin with twinkling eyes that flashed under tufted brows.

"You are the most notorious and celebrated jewel thief in the Near Stars," he said mildly. It was a statement, not a question. "It was Kirin of Tellus who stole the Nine Diamonds of Pharvis from the dragon-guarded citadel beside the Flaming Sea. It was you who carried off the tiara of the harlot Queen of Zodah, a trifle composed of eleven thousand matched fire-rubies, worth an emperor's ransom. That one was not so easy. You left eleven corpses behind you, but you were unharmed. And once, on Mnom the Dark World, you laughingly boasted you could steal the Twin Moons of Urnadon out of the skies, if somebody was willing to pay you a good enough price for them. Am I correct?"

"Very," Kirin said softly. He was relaxed but wary. The little fat man grinned suddenly, plump cheeks wobbling.

"I am no monitor, if that's what you're thinking! Space, no! In fact, I—uh—in my secular days before I joined the Order, I was, ahem, a bit of a thief myself over on Onaldus and Nar." The doctor sighed nostalgically. "Ah, lad, those were the days…"

"Keep going," Kirin said.

"Hem! Well then. I came to Zha not only to keep those vile little monsters from scragging you, but to make you a proposition. I want you to steal something for me. A treasure. A jewel, in fact. It is very well and cunningly guarded, and the task requires a man of your calibre and adeptness. The jewel is on the planet Pelizon, where it is watched and guarded by the Death Dwarves, who regard it as a holy object. Somehow the cunning devils learned of our—of my—intent, and, to forestall it, planned to assassinate you so the jewel could not be stolen. I came to Zha to protect you from them. Unfortunately, I came by a freighter. I bought passage with the trader Baphomer. He has a slow ship and I was almost too late…"

Kirin digested this in silence. On the surface, at least, it made sense. But underneath, lay large unanswered questions.

"Temujin… Doctor Temujin, I believe you said. Doctor of what? And where exactly are you from?"

Temujin pursed his lips unhappily.

"I was rather hoping you would not ask that question," he wheezed, "but I am permitted to answer it. I am a doctor of the Minor Thaumaturgies and I am from Trevelon."

Trevelon? Curiouser and curiouser! Kirin had heard of that distant mysterious world. The "Planet of Philosophers," they called it in the Near Stars. But Kirin knew the grey sages of Trevelon were reputed to be more magicians than philosophers. They of Trevelon were masters of the lesser magics and meddled not at all with the doings of the worlds about them. They did not encourage visits and they never visited other worlds themselves. How odd, then, that the Master Mages of Trevelon should become embroiled in thievery, secret treasures and murder...

"Thaumaturgy," he grunted. "Then you are yourself a magician?"

Temujin preened his piratical mustachios and nodded.

"Aye, but the least and lowest of the mages," he confessed. "A few small talents, nothing more..."

Kirin said, "Well, if you people know my reputation you must also know that I am a lone wolf. I work on my own; I never accept assignments."

Temujin nodded unhappily.

"Exactly what I told the Elder Brothers," he puffed. "But they pointed out that you should be badly in need of funds by now and probably spoiling for some action after three months of rotting in the jungles of Zha. They instructed me to give you this—" He undipped a fat purse from his waistband and tossed it over to Kirin, who caught it and pulled the drawstring. A pool of glittering fire poured out into his cupped palm. He sucked in his breath just a little. Pyroliths! The fabulous pyroliths of Chandala were rare and precious... and there were enough of the self-luminous firestones in that bag to purchase a princedom!

"—And this," Temujin wheezed, handing over a sheaf of thick parchment, folded many times. The crisp paper crackled as Kirin opened the sheets and leafed through them curiously.

"The jewel we are after is called the Medusa," Temujin wheezed, settling back. "It is concealed within a structure called the Iron Tower which lies amidst the barren wastes of the uplands, guarded by a maze of traps and deadfalls. We have, over centuries, and at frightful labor, obtained very precise and complete blueprints of the Tower. As you can see from those drawings, there is one safe route through the obstacles and hazards. It is clearly marked in red. There will be no danger. No danger at all..."

Kirin had to admit that everything looked to be in order. If the blueprints were correct, it should be child's play to penetrate the magical defenses of the Iron Tower and steal the Medusa for the philosophers of Trevelon. The price was munificent and the project sounded exciting. But there were still a few unanswered questions that bothered him.

If it was so simple and easy, why did the Master Mages hire his services for so princely a fee, instead of performing the theft themselves? And for that matter, what was the Medusa anyway, and why did the Mages want it?

The softly modulated voice of the ship interrupted his thoughts.

"I have been under attack for the past 12.03 seconds," the ship observed calmly.

Kirin jumped, spilled his drink, snarled a curse, and rapped: "What kind of an attack?"

"Energy weapons," the ship murmured. "Two spaceships are in orbit with me. My deflector screens are thus far capable of sustaining the assault, which is in the gamma-ray frequencies, but my logic machines anticipate the use of disruptor tightbeams within a few more seconds."

"Break orbit and take evasive action," Kirin growled. Then, to the startled Temujin, "Must be those damned little dwarves again!" Raising his voice a trifle he said, "Ship! While you're at it, you might as well pick a course to Pelizon and get moving."

The die, as the ancient pre-space saying has it, was cast. And Kirin was on his way to steal the Medusa from the Iron Tower of Pelizon.

He had, of course, no slightest inkling that the fate of a thousand stars hung balanced on his decision…

CHAPTER 3

SPACE TRAP

Zha and Pelizon lay at opposite ends of the Wyvern Cluster, that group of several hundred suns that formed what was known as the Near Stars. Pelizon was a lonely little world on the further fringe, just beyond the Dragon Stars. Kirin commanded the ship to chart a course for Pelizon and settled down to study the blueprints of the Tower while the ship took care of everything else.

The ship was a superb example of the engineering miracles the Old Empire had been capable of. The New Empire was now building ships again, yes, and technology was on the rise, with new articles such as the rain-repelling weather-cloak Kirin had worn on Zha and his power gun. But even the technarchs of Valdamar could not create anything like Kirin's ship.

Scarcely a hundred yards from prow to stern, it was as sleek and trim and swift a craft as ever plied the dark cold wastes between the stars. It was crammed with defensive and offensive equipment, remarkably well equipped for a small cruiser. Virtually a miniature fortress. And swift and nimble and elusive. At his command, it climbed above the complicated orbits of the nine moons of Zha and flashed out of the plane of the ecliptic—and vanished. Literally vanished.

For not only was the ship swift and strong, but in flight it could be rendered all but completely indetectible as well. A dense magnetic field could be built around the hull, a field whose lines of force were so powerful that they could bend even light rays around the ship, thus rather effectively making Kirin's ship invisible to sight and to radar as well.

But there were other ways of detecting a ship in space. One was neutrino-emission; a star drive leaked neutrinos all over the place. Again, the Ancients had wrought cleverly and well. Kirin's ship was fitted with a brace of neutrino-baffles that blocked heavy particle seepage to an irreducible minimum. In fact, about the only thing the ship could not disguise was its basic mass. Luckily, only naval warships of the Omega class carried mass detectors. They were not only immense and very heavy but delicate as well, and there were only a few Omega-class warships in the Near Stars.

So to all intents and purposes, when the ship lifted out of Zha's solar system it vanished into thin air... thin space, rather.

Which made it all the more peculiar when the ship was attacked.

The first thing that happened was the brain went out of whack. The brain lost control of the ship. This was both remarkable, and alarming to boot—in fact, it was impossible.

The brain, a super-miniaturized computer robot of remarkable sophistication, supplied Kirin in lieu of a trained crew. It not only monitored the life support and power systems, but served as navigational computer and robot pilot as well, was programmed to interpret and act upon spoken commands and, lacking these, on its own judgment and the built-in Prime Directives.

* * * *

They were several hours out of Zha, relaxing over a late supper and getting to know one another a little better. While Kirin nursed a steaming cup of kaff, Temujin puffed on a small black oily pipe and was engaged in giving the thief some background information on the mysterious leader of the Death Dwarves.

"Frankly, lad, we know little about him," Temujin was saying. "He came out of nowhere to enter the ranks of the cult, and once in, rapidly climbed to a position of dominant power. But he's no Pelizonese, that's for certain. He's nearly seven feet tall and gaunt as a skeleton."

"Facial characteristics?" Kirin inquired.

"Space knows, lad! Goes masked behind a bit o' cloth—probably to make himself seem more mysterious. Calls himself Zarlak. The assassins call him 'the Veiled One' and think he is a prophet sent by their gods to lead them to greatness and power. All very odd and mystifying..."

"Then it was Zarlak who gave the command to have me killed?"

"Most likely. But we think there's a bit more to it beyond just wantin' to keep you from stealing the gem. We think Zarlak is after it himself."

"Hmm. Just what is this Medusa thing, anyway, Temujin? Is it just a jewel or something more."

Temujin winked mysteriously and laid a finger alongside his bulbous nose. "Something more, much more," he hissed in a conspiratorial tone. "A talisman of great power... very dangerous in the wrong hands. Trevelon has known about it for ages, but so long as it was guarded by the superstitious Death Dwarves and protected behind the magical safeguards of the Tower, we cared but little. But now that Zarlak the Veiled One has appeared on the scene, we have become a mite worried. We suspect that Zarlak knows the secret of the Medusa, and is on Pelizon for the sole purpose of getting his hands on it. Hence your assignment to steal the thing. Trevelon wants it primarily so that it may be destroyed and thus kept out of malevolent hands. It could be very dangerous if it fell into the possession of unscrupulous persons…"

"Kirin."

The ship spoke softly. The voder was set to emit a quiet, gently modulated tone, but somehow urgency rasped in the ship's mechanical voice.

"What is it?"

"I am being interfered with," the ship said calmly. "Some external source of power is attempting to gain control of my circuits."

The news was astonishing. Kirin almost spilled his kaff. He jumped up.

"What? But—that's impossible!"

"I know," the ship replied, "but that's what's happening."

"Where are we, anyway?"

"Passing through the edge of the Dragon Stars at the moment. We are almost to Pelizon," the ship replied. Its voice sounded a trifle slower and duller now.

"Where is the beam coming from—a ship?" Kirin demanded. Of course he was thinking of the two ships that had attacked him in orbit above Zha. But how could the Death Dwarves track him through interstellar space? It was impossible… but, come to think of it, no more impossible than for the ship to be detected in space at all.

"No, the beam is planet-based, I feel certain. From the background resonance I can sense a planetary magnetic field… I am trying to track the beam, but it is very difficult… Kirin. I have lost control of my navigational computer components. We are veering onto another course. We are heading for…"

And then the brain went silent.

And stayed silent.

* * * *

Kirin groaned a curse and Temujin looked pale and grim. No longer under control, the ship hurtled off on a wild tangent which carried it far off course. But—where was it headed?

Kirin dialed the forward visors and stared into a glittering sea of stars. He could make no sense out of the groupings. A planet-bound observer learns to identify stars by the shape of the constellations. But in deep space, constellations change beyond all recognition when viewed from different angles, and space travelers find visual memory of as little use as a signpost. With the brain inoperative and the navigational computers under exterior control, Kirin had no way of telling where he was or where he was going, except for the one valid set of interstellar signposts, the spectra of the stars themselves. For while very many of the suns of space fall into certain common spectral types, there are a few prominent stars of very unusual spectrum, and a lost spacefarer can sometimes chart his course by spectroscopic analysis alone.

Luckily, the spectroscope was under manual controls, so Kirin unlimbered it and took a look around. As would commonly be the case in any given portion of the galactic spiral, there were a preponderance of Main Sequence stars of common spectra: B5's like Achernar, K5 Red Giants like Aldebaran, and a sprinkling of G2 stars like Sol. He moved the 'scope around and before long located a very unusual three-component multiple star. The brightest of the three was a B8, the second was a yellow-white G0 star, and the third, very dim, was an F5. The first two stars revolved around a common center of gravity, and the third of the group revolved about the other two with a period of what Kirin roughly estimated with the 'scope calculator to be some twenty-one months.

He had found Algol. No other triple sun remotely like this was to be found in the Near Stars. Now he needed one more reference point.

He found two without any trouble: Ross 614, a binary star composed of two Red Dwarves, and the unmistakable superbeacon of S Doradus in the Core Stars of the Greater Magellanic Cloud. Although outside of the galaxy proper, S Doradus was visible in the 'scope due to its extraordinary nature. This eclipsing binary, made up of two Blue Giants, was one of the most unusual stars known to man. Each of the two suns which made up the binary system were hundreds of thousands of times more bright than Sol. In fact, the first component, S Doradus A was a good half a million times brighter than an ordinary Main Sequence star and was the intrinsically brightest star known to man. There was no mistaking S Doradus…

With these three reference points to work from, it was not long before Kirin had formed a good idea of their location and the direction in which they were traveling. They were in the Dragon Stars, headed off Rim-wards virtually at a right angle to their original course. Every moment took them further from Pelizon. If they continued on their present path, they would head completely out of the Near Stars and be in unknown regions.

But since they were helpless to alter the ship's direction, or to regain control, there was nothing they could do about it.

* * * *

After a time they slept. The small cabin had two bunks built into opposite walls. Kirin took his usual bunk and fat old Temujin stretched out in the other. While they slept, the ship surged on its mysterious course, penetrating deeper and deeper into the Dragon Stars.

After several hours, it emerged from the Interplenum— that paradoxical artificial universe wherein a ship may travel at enormous multiples of the speed of light without any increase of mass—and re-entered normal space. A huge world loomed ahead of them, vast and dreary, with continent-wide deserts of ochre sand, and twelve moons lighting its velvet skies.

Although Kirin did not know it, this was Zangrimar, lone planet of the star Solphis in the Dragon Stars. A barren wilderness world, a jumble of broken rock in the highlands, else a vast dying world of bitter sands scoured by howling winds. Naught dwelt in the wide wastes but sluggish lizards that fed upon purple moss.

The surge of power, when the ship passed into normal space, awoke Kirin. The drone of the drive was lower and thicker now, and he knew they were on planetary power. Awaking the snoring doctor, he sprinted to the forward visors and snapped them on. Zangrimar was a dull glowing crescent, rising into their vision even as he watched. His jaw tightened grimly.

"Well, we're here," he growled. "Wherever 'here' may be!"

Without a hand at the controls, fully under the power of the strange force trap that had seized them in midflight, the ship dropped through the thin atmosphere of the desert world. Kirin could see a weird metal city built on a high plateau. Sunfire flashed from angles, planes and mirror-bright surfaces.

He wondered if yet a third party was interested in the Medusa…

The ship landed gently in a hollow cradle. Power died. Eyeing the atmospheric analysis dials beside the lock, he discovered the air outside was thin, cold, but breathable.

So he went outside to wait for the reception committee. There was nothing else he could do... for the moment...

He did not have long to wait. But it was Temujin who saw them first. Wheezing at the exertion, the red-faced little thaumaturge clambered out of the lock to stand beside him on the gleaming metallic surface of the space field. He stared around, blinking owlishly at the strange metal buildings. They were built to fantastic designs, weird pagodas, terraced pyramids and soaring ziggurats of glittering steel. Colossal steel masks glowered down at them from tower-tops, the sides of domes, the architraves of long arcades. Eyes of red fire blazed from the cruel metal masks.

The clank of metal striking on metal came to their ears. Across the space field came a blurred group of towering figures. Temujin spotted them and yelped.

"Robots!" he shrilled.

An unearthly chill crawled up Kirin's spine. He looked at the metal colossi that came stalking up to them. Their heads were like the enormous casques of helmeted warriors. Long jointed arms ended in cruel steel claws. Nine feet from toe to crown the steel giants towered. They looked like mailed warriors out of nightmares.

Across the field in a straight file they came directly for the two men. With a sinking heart, Kirin realized they had no hope of defending themselves. They were prisoners, on an unknown world...

CHAPTER 4

THE WITCH QUEEN

The metal giants were unearthly, terrifying. Kirin had heard of their like before. The old Carina Imperials had been served by metal slaves. Mechanical men had performed much of the common labor of the Empire. And it was said that certain of the steel automata were invested with extraordinary intelligence, some were as clever and articulate as men. But, being metal, it was a cold unyielding intelligence, devoid of mercy, warmth, humanity, or humor.

From the looks of them, the steel giants were over a thousand years old. It was astonishing to realize that the metal men still survived, still lived and labored and thought, centuries after the Empire that had created them had fallen into dust. But so it was. Surely, modern science could not produce such metal phenomena. They must be survivors of an earlier age…

"What shall we do, lad?" old Temujin quavered, striving manfully to still his trembling limbs. "Fight them?"

Kirin was tempted, but it was hopeless. There were too many. His power gun and the old doctor's mysterious ivory rod could perhaps account for a few, but a few were not enough. Besides, even if they could fight free, the ship was still held under the control of whatever intelligence ruled this city of shimmering steel, be it man or metal. It would be the wisest course to go along with their captors, to learn why they had been forced down on this forbidding world, to discover the identity and purpose of their unknown enemy, before striking for freedom. He shook his head.

"No, Doc. Let's go quietly."

His voice was low and steady. Temujin bristled, half-raised the gleaming ivory tube that was his only weapon, then subsided into grumbling under his breath. Kirin suppressed a chuckle. The fat little old man was short of breath, but long on courage. Although obviously he was terrified of the approaching metal warriors, his instinct was to do battle. Bristling his bandit mustachios and glaring like an infuriated war-horse, the little magician snorted himself into silence. Kirin knew what he felt like... he didn't like to give in without a fight either. But the thief had learned many lessons in the past—some of them painful. He had learned not to rely so much on sheer force, brute strength, or battling skill. These were all very well, but subtlety and cunning and a keen, vigilant eye often proved the strongest in the long run.

Casting back to a scrap of antique, pre-space literature he had once perused, Kirin was reminded of the battle of Troy. It was not the heroic strength of Achilles that breached the mighty walls of the fabulous city, but the subtle cunning of sly Odysseus.

He permitted himself to be captured.

* * * *

In a distant part of the metal city, in a high-ceilinged chamber hung with velvet curtains of mystic green and lit by a small ruby lamp, a woman of exotic beauty observed Kirin and Temujin as they permitted themselves to be captured.

Her almond-shaped eyes, veiled in dark lashes, narrowed thoughtfully as she let her gaze run slowly over the lean hard body of the stalwart Earthling. Kirin and

Temujin were mirrored within a curved globe of polished crystal. It was like a miniature scene cast by a video projector in three dimensions. Although no sounds issued from the glittering crystal, it was otherwise true to life down to the minutest of details.

In the soft daylight glow from the crystal, which stood on a pillar of grey stone, her face was like that of some goddess peering down on the small and trivial doings of men. Masklike were her features; the incredible perfection of her beauty making her face look more like a superb work of art than a human visage, for no emotions flowed across the sculpture of her face; calm and cold she stared down, and only the dark fires of her slanting eyes denoted life and intelligence.

She was tall and slender and deliciously rounded, her body a poem of warm silken flesh, which the daring cut of her gown revealed to best advantage. The dark glittering cloth of her robe clung silkenly to every seductive curve. Her flesh, copiously revealed in the low-cut and sleeveless raiment, was lustrous and tinted jade green. Her hair was black as space itself and loosely coiled atop her head, threaded through with minute diamonds that flashed like cold stars amidst her night-black locks. Her lips were full and generous, moist, a dark soft emerald. A slight smile lay upon them as she let her gaze linger on the tall Earthling.

To her companion she said, "The little fat man is of Trevelon from his grey robe; I have seen his like before. But the tall man with dark skin and hawk-like, bitter face, what is he? I have never seen hair like that before, nor a man with that stance of lonely pride…"

"Kirin is from Tellus," the man said softly. "The third planet of the star Sol in Central Orion. Some say it is the home-world from which man spread into space ten thousand years ago; others say Centaurus; others, Tau Ceti. It makes little difference, but it is interesting to speculate…"

She flashed him a venomous glance of cold mockery from her jewel-bright eyes, "That is what you do best, Pangoy, in fact, all you can do is speculate! You Nexians bore me. You are too cold and clever." Her companion bowed beneath the lash of scorn in her voice. The woman glanced into the glowing crystal again and her voice became languorous and caressing, "Now, if I had such a man as that by my side… what might the two of us not accomplish, with time?"

The man watched her from impassive eyes as she stared into the crystal. He was tall and gaunt, with saffron skin and dark suave eyes, dressed in a loose robe of purple velvet. The symbol of a crimson dragon was stitched into the cloth above his heart. Hair was shaven from his polished skull. He was more than seven centuries old, as one might guess from the network of tiny, almost invisible wrinkles that meshed his face. His immortality was derived from an annual injection of pituitary fluid drawn from human infants. He was one of the Mind Wizards of Nex, and had come to Zangrimar twenty years ago to destroy the woman who now stood beside him by the crystal. Instead, she had conquered and enslaved him, as she had enslaved every other living thing on this planet. But he was a willing slave, the unslaked fire of desire that blazed in his cold reptilian eyes when he watched her gave the reason…

"Azeera, my Queen," he murmured, "I feel you are entering into a dangerous endeavor. It is enough that we shall earn the enmity of Zarlak and the Death Dwarves when we make our attempt to steal the Medusa, now you would pit us against the Master Mages of Trevelon as well! I begin to regret that I ever lent the aid of my mental powers and assisted you in unlocking the Vault of Time…"

"However, you did. And look at the marvels we have uncovered," the Queen said coldly. She made a gesture and the picture vanished within the crystal, its fires dimming. She turned away and mounted black jade steps to a throne of rose-tinted ivory set under a canopy of that iridescent crystal-cloth spun by the sentient Arachnidae of Algol IV. Stretching like a lazy cat, she settled herself therein and sprawled, toying with a blazing jewel, watching him with cold cruel eyes wherein mockery flashed.

"A century ago when I came to this planet I realized it must be one of the long-forgotten Science Worlds," she murmured. "I discovered this metal city and learned how to awaken the metal warriors from their centuries-old slumber. With them bound to my will, I conquered the humans who had long dwelt on this bleak and barren world, never daring to disturb the sleeping terrors of the metal city. I made them my slaves, and the city of the Ancients became my capital. I knew the lost Science Worlds had never been discovered. I knew the Ancients left their laboratories and wisdom-vaults concealed and locked when the Empire collapsed. I deduced that the robot warriors were here to guard such a vault. Together, you and I, we found it and opened it. And now we stand on the threshold of power beyond limit. The force field we used to capture the Earthman's ship was but one of the incredible science-miracles the Ancients hid away in the sealed vault beneath this city. When we have learned how to master all the other wonder machines therein, I shall truly become Empress of the star worlds…"

He said quietly, "I have said it before and I repeat it now, my Queen. With the treasures of the Vault at our command, we do not need the Medusa. And we stray into dangerous paths in attempting to secure it..."

Her eyes flashed cold fires. "So, Pangoy! You would have me begin my march of conquest without the Medusa? You would have me launch my robot legions against the Inner Worlds, knowing that the wise men of Trevelon will oppose me as they oppose every would-be conqueror? Knowing that Trevelon can use the Medusa against me? Knowing what the Medusa is?"

He shook his head. "Nay, you distort my words. I know the dread power of the Medusa. I know that it almost conquered the Universe aeons ago, ere the god Valkyr sealed it within the Iron Tower. But what I advise is this, launch your robot armada against Trevelon first. Demolish it, before you hurl your might against the Inner Worlds. Then the Medusa cannot be used against you, for the malignant little Death Dwarves do not know how to gain entry into the Iron Tower as that impostor, Zarlak, must have learned by now."

She stirred restlessly. "I am not ready to challenge the magic of Trevelon," she said.

He smiled gently. "Precisely. You are not even ready to launch your invasion of the Inner Worlds. Why, then, seize this fat little mage and the Earthling and thus bring yourself to the attention of Trevelon and Zarlak? Thus far both factors have ignored our existence. They know you are the tyrant of Zangrimar, and they know something of your power, but you pose as yet no menace to the star worlds—as far as they know. They cannot know you have opened the Time Vault and found the scientific treasures of the Old Empire. They cannot know that you energized the Space Mirror and thus have been able to observe their councils and to learn of the power of the Medusa and their plans to steal it before Zarlak does, so that it may be immobilized or destroyed. But with this action, you enter a great game openly. No longer can we work in secret."

There was no denying the logic in his soft purring voice, but Azeera stirred restively under his words.

"Yes, yes, Pangoy, I know all this. But it is too late to argue your point further. If I do not interfere now, and use Kirin to steal the gem for me, then Trevelon or Zarlak will get it, and they will be able to use it against me when my legions are ready to attack. It is they who have, unknowingly, forced my hand! But in any case, the thing is done. It is too late for words. Now leave me!"

Pangoy sighed. As always, they argued from irreconcilable positions. He bowed, and padded out of the green-hung chamber, leaving the Witch Queen to brood on her ivory throne alone.

* * * *

The metal giants escorted Kirin and Temujin through the winding ways of the glittering city. Everywhere they saw about them evidence of tremendous industry. Automatic factories were humming, turning out sky sleds and energy weapons and star ships. Throngs of the metal warriors moved through the streets, bound on mysterious errands. Sleds dipped, hovered, circled through the sky above the city like steel insects. The fantastic metal towers of the strange city blazed with light.

They even saw people. But very few. Obviously, the human inhabitants of this unknown planet were vastly outnumbered by the giant robots. The few they glimpsed while being escorted from the space field looked pale and wan, with frightened eyes and bent shoulders. The metal warriors were the masters here, that much was obvious.

They were ushered into one of the flying sleds. It was an oval platform of glittering metal some ten feet long, with a guardrail about its perimeter. One of the robots stationed himself at the control chair before a low pedestal of gleaming crystal wherein small lights flickered. He manipulated the surface of the pedestal in a certain manner and Kirin watched his actions closely without seeming to. It occurred to him that if they were later to make their escape from the metal metropolis, it might prove useful to know how to pilot one of the sky sleds. The mechanism looked simple enough to operate.

The oval platform lifted weightlessly off the ground and went skimming into the air. Invisible pressor beams emitted from the lower surface lifted and drove the craft smoothly. Kirin watched the robot's metal fingers as they sped over the crystal surface of the control device. He saw how it was driven.

The sky sled swooped between mile-tall towers of glass and steel. It soared above congested roadways and over aerial networks of bridges, heading for the heart of the ancient city. Kirin knew this must be one of the centuries-ago abandoned cities of the Empire, somehow miraculously preserved undamaged and operable since the collapse of the Carina regnum a thousand years before. But were humans in charge here, or had the robot warriors ruled throughout the centuries since the Empire fell? From the worn, pale, frightened faces of the few humans he had seen, it seemed likely the metal men were in command...

Towards the center of the city rose a colossal citadel. This, obviously, from its central and prominent position, was the seat of power. They hurtled towards it and as they drew nearer, Kirin's keen eyes could see the legions of metal men guarding every approach to the central citadel. Pale beams of light flickered from roof and dome and grounds, a force-fence, obviously, guarding against chance entry or insurrection. His heart sank within him. Perhaps it would have been wiser to have fought against capture. They were heading for what looked to be an impregnable fortress. It would be a hard place to escape from…

But he comforted himself with the thought that he was Kirin of Tellus, and the greatest thief in the Near Stars. He had broken into many places just as well guarded. With the miniature implements of his thieving trade, which he wore ever concealed on his person, and his knowledge of doors and locks, he had often boasted that no fortress was impenetrable where he was concerned.

Of course, this would be the first time he had ever had to use his skills to break out of a fortress…

The sky sled skimmed above the palace grounds and came to a gentle landing atop one tier of the towering citadel. A steel phalanx of guards closed about Kirin and the doctor and guided them into the frowning bastion of a massive gate.

The steel doors closed behind them. There was a certain grim note of finality to the sound, as they clanged shut.

CHAPTER 5

THE HALL OF SPHINXES

The cell into which the metal warriors thrust Kirin and Doctor Temujin was luxurious rather than merely comfortable. Walls of priceless winewood panelling from the Garden Worlds met their eyes. The floor was tiled with alternate squares of green and yellow marble, and glowing tapestry-carpets were scattered about it. Silken divans met their gaze, and low tabourets of rare woods bore bowls of bright flowers. From a brazen tripod a wavering spiral of pale green scented smoke perfumed the air. Kirin sniffed appreciatively. It was an exquisite blend of burnt cinnamon and white spikenard from Dolmentus.

"Now this is what I call a jail!" he grinned. Temujin looked about glumly.

"It may be comfortable, lad," he wheezed dispiritedly, "but it is still a prison. Alas!" He sank wearily on one of the soft divans and clasped his fat red face in his hands. "I did not mention it before, but I am not particularly in favor with the Elder Brothers of my order back on Trevelon," he groaned. "To expiate my sins I was given this important mission; if I performed it well, all would be forgiven. Alas, things could not have gone worse... and now the mission is ended and all is lost. Woe is me . . . woe . . . !"

Kirin laughed and clapped the little man on one bowed shoulder.

"Cheer up, Doc. Things are not as bad as that, and they may get better soon. After all, whoever rules this place could have chained us into a dark cold dungeon.

Obviously, from this kind of treatment, he or they want us in good health, or they wouldn't be treating us so well. Never give up, old fellow!"

A gleam shone in the magician's eye.

"Why do you say things may get better soon?" he inquired. "Do you have a plan?"

"Maybe," Kirin grinned.

"You think you can get us out of here, lad? But how? They took your gun—they even took my Rod of Power! We are unarmed and among enemies…"

He broke off as Kirin suddenly gestured for silence. The door was opening. Kirin tensed, expecting one of the towering metal colossi, instead it was a young girl who entered the room bearing a tray of food. He looked her over with appreciation. She was well worth looking at. Slim and blond, with hair like spun gold and wide bold eyes of emerald green. She had a lush figure and long sinuous legs and a ripe mouth made for kissing. Her abbreviated garment, breastplates of silver, silver slippers, and a silken loin-cloth, did little to hide her loveliness. She looked about eighteen.

"So they aren't all made of metal in this place, eh?" Kirin grinned. She flashed him a bold look from tip-tilted green eyes as she set the tray down on a low table of candle-wood. Dishes of savory meat and hot pastries and a bowl of mixed fruits lay thereon, and a flagon of wine.

"We saw a few people in the streets as we entered the city," Kirin said, "but they all looked pale and beaten. You look very different, girl. What's your name?"

"Caola," she said softly. "Caola of Nar. I am a palace slave, and hence better treated than the city folk," she said. "But I am not supposed to talk to you, and she may be listening!"

"Who is 'she'—the ruler of this city?" Kirin asked.

But the girl was gone swiftly, indicating that she dare not talk with them any longer.

"If that's the sort of maids they have in this hotel," Kirin mused appreciatively as he sat down to lunch, "I won't mind staying here a while."

Temujin only groaned and put his head in his hands.

"Have some wine and cheer up, Doc," the thief advised. The old magician shook his head dolefully.

"Don't remind me of the stuff!" he sighed. "It was because of my fondness for the fluid that my Order disciplined me in the first place... well, perhaps just a drop," he wheezed. Kirin poured him a full goblet.

"Just for medicinal purposes, mind you," the old magician said lamely, in answer to Kirin's mocking grin.

* * * *

It was many hours later when the metal men came for them. Kirin cautioned his companion against any rash words or hasty actions.

"Just look and listen," he said tersely. "Leave the talking to me. But keep your eyes open. Everything we can learn about this setup could be valuable, you never know when an odd bit of information may come in handy later on."

The old thaumaturge growled dubiously and whuffed through his bandit mustachios, but ambled along behind Kirin as the robot guards escorted them out of the room. They passed through corridors and chambers of surpassing beauty. Thousands of different kinds of stone were fitted together into a mosaic of contrasts. Lime-green Vegan marble and yellow Argionid granite and milky, lucent silkstone from the Ghost Moon. Sleek blue stone of Irian quarries and that blood-red alabaster the Tigermen mine from the desert hills of Bartosca, snarling under the lash of the Winged People who are their lords. The effect was exquisite and subtle.

At length they entered into a tremendous hall whose groined and vaulted ceiling was lost in murky shadows far over their heads. Mighty sphinxes of dark smooth stone were ranked the length of this hall, and green glowing jewelled eyes flashed in the dark enigma of their faces. A feast was in progress in the sphinx-lined hall; it hummed with soft conversation, which stilled upon their entrance. Kirin's gaze flew past the silk-clad lords and their veiled ladies, to study the slim, languorous woman who sat enthroned above the throng. She was ravishing, the flawless beauty of her jade green arms and bare shoulders set off by a high-necked gown of glittering silver cloth. A jewelled tiara crusted with pale red diamonds blazed in her silken tresses, the hue of midnight. Fiery dark eyes like black stars caught and held his own.

Beside him, Kirin sensed the fat thaumaturge start suddenly.

"Gods of Space," Temujin breathed, "I have heard of that woman! There cannot be two of them in this galaxy. She is Azeera, the Witch Queen!"

"So we are on Zangrimar, the lone planet of the star Solphis," Kirin mused. But every eye was upon them and they had no time for further talk. The Witch Queen beckoned imperiously and guards led them to places set on the dais near her throne chair.

"Come, my honored guests, and join our festivities," she called, and her voice was low, throaty, alluring. Kirin tried to make a jest out of the contrast between her words and the fact that they had been forced down and held under guard, but his usual wit deserted him and his tongue stumbled over the words. Azeera watched him with a mingling of amusement and cool appraisal. There was also a certain admiration in her eyes. Temujin felt inward qualms and sought to warn his young comrade to be on guard against the wiles of the woman, but Kirin acted rather like one in a daze and seemed not to hear.

Temujin gave up trying and fell to the sumptuous meal. From all that he had heard of the green lady of Zangrimar, Kirin would not be the first man who had fallen under the dazzling spell of her seductive loveliness.

The feast, he was reluctantly forced to admit, was superb. A succession of young female slaves, dressed much in the same manner of abbreviated garment as the girl Caola had worn, presented an assortment of delicious dishes from which the guests lazily selected their portions. Great platters of chased gold, electrum, silver and sparkling chaya bore succulent roast moon-ox, broiled shynx with Vegan cloves, rare Pharvisian snow-tiger steak, steaming dumplings in herb gravy, and all manner of fantastical pastries and delicacies crusted with sugar and preserved fruits and jellies.

Temujin fell to with a hearty appetite and downed an enormous meal, washed down with a succession of beverages. There were the green wines of Shazar and Bellerophon, and rich red-golden ales from Netharna and Chorver, and fiery purple Valthomé liquor, and chilled goblets of sparkling neol, and yet others to sample. The queer wines and liqueurs of half a hundred worlds were here for the asking.

Chewing a savory slice of Chadorian venison in rich spice-cream sauce, Temujin resigned himself to captivity, with the thought that if all prisons served so regal a fare as this, few men would seek freedom!

Azeera engaged Kirin in conversation. Generally, the thief had a suave and witty way with women. But this radiant and mysterious creature filled him with awe. He could hardly take his eyes off her, or stop listening to the honeyed and seductive music of her warm, purring voice. She exuded a heavy intoxicating aura of sexual allure that was almost overpowering. His eyes clung to her slim bare arms, to the rich curve of hip and thigh, to the sleek, ripe globes of her swelling breasts. He hardly tasted the food or the exquisite wines that were set before him.

Despite her allure, the Earthman strove to keep his wits about him. It seemed obvious that the Witch Queen used the power of her body, the spell of her voice, and the dark sorcery of her eyes to conquer men, and he battled against these seductive magics with all the manhood within him. He found himself wondering at the lovely girls who served the feast—only a woman confident of her own superb beauty would dare surround herself with such charming young slaves. He dwelled upon the insolence implied in this kind of over-weening self-confidence. It suggested a clue to the nature of Azeera; perhaps even a flaw in her defenses. If he could resist her blandishments, disdain them…

"Let me ask, my lady, for a simple answer to a simple question," he proposed bluntly. Anything to end this verbal parrying and to get to the point. "My companion and I are curious as to your reasons for forcing our ship down on your world."

Her almond eyes glinted with jewelled fires.

"Very well, then," she said softly. "A simple answer it shall be. I, too, want to hire you to steal the Medusa."

He started, but controlled his reaction, hoping that his astonishment was not visible on his face. Before he could think of something to say, she continued.

"Let us abandon all this subterfuge," Azeera said. "I need you for the same reason Trevelon needs you. Only to a thief of your calibre do I dare entrust so vital a mission. A lesser man might falter and fail, attempting to penetrate the magical defenses that guard the Iron Tower from intruders. Failure can be fatal to my plans, for it will alert the Death Dwarves and the watchers of Trevelon. There can only be one attempt on the Medusa, and I dare not risk failure."

"What is it about this jewel that makes it so important to so many people?" he mused. She pounced upon the question as a cat might pounce upon a small rodent who had thoughtlessly exposed itself.

"Ah, so the wise men of Trevelon did not tell you that secret, eh?" she laughed, eyes bright with witch-fires of mockery. "I wonder that you trust the grey philosophers, since they obviously do not trust you. Well, I will hold no secrets from you, Kirin of Tellus. The Medusa is the most important thing in the Universe. It is the key to power. With it, one may stretch out his hand and pluck the star worlds like gems to form an Imperial coronet."

She rose, and the room fell silent. Slim and unbearably lovely in the shimmering gown of metallic silver, she stood like a statuette cast by a master hand from precious metals.

"Come with me, Kirin of Tellus, and I will put into your hands the Secret of the Universe. Come with me … if you dare!"

Her voice rang through the silent vastness of the hall of sphinxes like a war horn, summoning legions to victory.

The sirenic witchery of her voice reached out and stirred to life something deep within him, a central core of emotion, a hungering after heroic deeds, a lust for fame and glory, whose existence he had never suspected. He thrilled to the ringing music of her voice and the dark fire within her slanting eyes, and rose numbly to his feet although the fat little thaumaturge plucked feebly at his arm and sought to stay him. He brushed the hand aside impatiently, shrugged off the half-heard protests of the little man. Glory summoned him to high, heroic deeds of valor! And he must respond.

"Lead on, lady," he said huskily. "And I will come with you…"

Together they left the hall.

Across the dais, seated at a long low table, the shadowy form of the bald Mind Wizard, Pangoy, of Nex, watched them go, with sardonic eyes and a slight mirthless smile that did not hide the bitter agony in his heart. The woman had found a new toy to play with, to mold to her purpose, to fondle for a time, before she cast it broken in the dust…

His eyes narrowed. Not for nothing had the Witch Queen studied the twin arts of semantics and sonics. Her voice became a tool and a weapon of extraordinary subtlety and power. Already the Earthling was enslaved…

CHAPTER 6

THE HEART OF KOM YAZOTH

It was a titanic sphere, seven times the height of a man. A silvery mesh formed the substance of the colossal globe that floated on pressor beams above the floor of the black marble chamber. The mesh of wires were woven with such fineness that they were all but invisible to the sight; only in their mass were they visible. Hence, the sphere seemed as a cloudy globe of dim grey mist, shadowy, insubstantial, awesome.

"I call this the Space Mirror," Azeera said. "I know not what the Ancients named it, but the term will suffice. It was the first of the great treasures I drew from the hidden Vault of Time wherein its masters sealed it a thousand years ago. It is one of the mightiest accomplishments of the science-magic of the Carina Imperials. Through the power of the Mirror, one can gaze at events taking place in any part of the Universe, on any world, no matter how remote from us here. No walls can resist the probing gaze of the Space Mirror. No councils are so secret that I may not eavesdrop upon them through the magic of this misty sphere. Behold!"

She pressed her jewelled ring against a column of milky crystal that rose from the ebon floor. Light flared! The silver mesh glowed with eerie luminance. Shadowy grey turned to a swimming sea of infinitesimal sparks of star-like light that throbbed brighter and brighter until they formed a whirling ball of silver fire. Then the silver globe flashed with a thousand hues… rose-pink and coral, peach gold and palest azure, a velvet blackness wherein emerald sparks burned like cat's eyes, shimmering mists of opal and mauve spun through with threads of rich crimson flame. And the colors wove into a tapestry that blurred, steadied, and crystallized into a vision so complete in every detail that Kirin shrank back a step, as if he stood before a yawning door through which a mis-step might hurl him to spinning worlds below.

The picture was now a scene of somber majesty and brooding terrors. No sound accompanied the space-vision, but the imagination of the viewer could almost hear the cold wind that shrieked like a banshee through the fang-sharp needle spires of naked rock that clawed up into the mist-veiled sky. There was a flat and barren plain, an endless desert of dim grey crystals that stretched from world's edge to world's edge. Over all stretched an eternal cloak of phantasmal fog, torn and tattered into a thousand leering faces and weirdly haunting shapes by the howling winds. The shadowy rags of mist streamed in undulant and serpentine tendrils above a titanic structure of dead black stone that loomed against the fog-phantoms like some colossal citadel of demons.

The black castle was unthinkably huge, immeasurably aged. A forest of sloping turrets and grotesquely-formed domes, a wilderness of arcades and columns, squat towers and yawning gates like the leering maws of nameless stone monsters. The chill, the eerie cry of endless winds, the haunting air of mouldering decay and aeon-old desolation struck awe into the very roots of Kirin's soul.

"That black castle is Djormandark Keep," the Witch Queen murmured at his side. But he did not need her words to tell him this, for no man could mistake the colossal ebon fortress. Djormandark was one of the enigmas of the Universe, and the very world whereon its titanic ruin reared its cloven, castled crest was known as the Planet of Mystery—dark, legend-fraught Xulthoom, the World of the Hooded Men.

The Space Mirror had somehow probed down through thousands of miles of dense mists to reveal the ever-hidden face of the mystery world. No radar, no sonic probe, no spy-ray known to the young science of this age could penetrate to the surface of Xulthoom. He stared at the fantastic scene with awe and amazement, and only now did he begin to grasp the power the Witch Queen held in her slim hands.

The scene changed in a blur of rainbow colors that made the eye ache.

Now he looked down as from the bridge of a star cruiser upon another land of desolate wilderness. From pole to pole the planet that next met his gaze was sheathed under a colossal glacier like a continent of crystal. The dull, glistening mirror blazed suddenly with uncanny brilliance. The planet revolved slowly against the tides of night, and a blinding glory sprang into being as it turned. A gigantic hand of fire flashed across the face of the deep. Tremendous streamers of incandescent splendor spanned the sky above the frozen world like rivers of fiery diamond dust. The glory of a billion dawns lit the glassy surface of the frigid world until it blazed like one colossal jewel of a million facets against the black velvet of the void.

And again he did not need her words to recognize the scene, although he had never looked upon it in all his days. This could only be Arlomma the Ice World, which clung like a crystal gem to the blazing breast of that titanic, luminous gas-cloud known as the Kraken Nebula. Arlomma lay far across the cluster from Zangrimar, beyond the Inner Worlds, beyond even Onaldus. Yet the mystery force of the Mirror had spanned a dozen light-leagues in the flash of a second!

The splendor died. The glory faded. The magic Mirror became again a dull, cloudy sphere of shadowy mesh.

* * * *

She led him to a seat beside her on a low bench of black jade. Her hand was on his arm. He could feel the warmth of her thigh against his leg, and the musky perfume she wore wove its spell in his brain. The insidious music of her voice murmured softly as he sat entranced.

"With the power of the Space Mirror I have explored worlds unknown to man and learned many ancient secrets," she said. "I will tell you one of them. It is a story, a legend, if you like. In the Beginning, the Children of the Fire Mist came from beyond the Universes into this realm of space. Whatever they were, and legend tells but little of them, they ruled our cosmos untold billions of years before the coming of Man. Life itself had not yet evolved into being upon the new worlds that spun about the young suns of this galaxy. They were not gods, although their powers were awesome and terrible. The gods, and there are indeed gods, and stranger and more amazing than the priests of the star worlds dare reveal—have but little to do with the Universes they created in the Dawn…"

Her voice was witch-music, whispering of mysteries and wonders almost beyond thought. Drowsily he listened to her low, warm voice.

"And then came a Thing from Beyond into this dimension of space. What it was and from whence it came, even legend does not tell. But the Children of the Fire Mist, for all their awesome command over the forces of nature and the power of time itself, even they were as helpless babes before the Unknown One. Kom Yazoth, they called it, which means in the Language of the Gods, The Conqueror of Souls, and they fled from its coming. For it was very old, and very powerful, and its power lay in this strange magic: it could seize utter and absolute control of any sentient being who beheld it, be he ne'er so mighty.

"The Children of the Fire Mist feared greatly the coming of this Demon-Thing from beyond the cosmos of space and time, for they were helpless to oppose it. In their inscrutable way and for purposes at which we may not even guess, they had caused to be born life on the young planets, and sentience arose and grew. But Kom Yazoth gained empery over the young worlds and the life thereon, until it seemed as if all the Universe would fall under the spell of the Demon.

"In their desperate and ultimate need, the Children of the Fire Mist fought the Transcosmic One, but Kom Yazoth broke them and whelmed their power and they fled from him and went back to that unknown realm from whence they had come before the Beginning, even to the Fire Mist itself which had spawned them in the immeasurable darkness before Time was.

"And at length, with the passing of the Children, the Gods themselves were troubled. They slumber eternal in their place beyond and above all the Universe, and rarely are they wakened from their indescribable dreams. But now they woke and saw the power of Kom Yazoth and knew that the Thing from Beyond must somehow be slain or driven from this Universe back into the ultimate abyss of darkness.

"So they sent forth from their shining number the mightiest of the Warrior Gods, even Valkyr the Invincible. And the golden Hero God strove long and mightily against the Demon, ever shielding his gaze from the dark

Thing that his will might not be taken from him. For were he, even he, the Champion of the Gods, to be overcome and fall into the uncanny slavery of the Conqueror of Souls, what hope had even the Gods of all the Universes that they could escape from the coming of The Insatiable One?

"Vast were the powers he unleashed against the Trans-cosmic Demon. Suns he wrenched from their stations to hurl against the terror of Kom Yazoth; nebulae flamed to life and galaxies were demolished in the aeon-long battle. Cosmic forces hurled against the Demon; the very underlying fabric of space itself was rent and torn with the colossal energies released in that greatest of battles...

"And the ending of it was, that in the fullness of time, Valkyr the Glorious slew the Demon, and destroyed him utterly, disintegrating the very substance whereof his form was wrought, so that there was naught of Kom Yazoth that remained.

"Except for his Heart.

"For the heart of a demon does not die easily and such as Kom Yazoth, devotees of Chaos, lords and princes of Ultracosmic Evil, have hearts that are cold and dead and frozen as a jewel. Thus was the Heart of Kom Yazoth like unto a great crystal. And therein resided yet a vestige of his awesome power to steal and dominate the mind and will and the very soul of all that looked thereupon.

"He who held the Heart could at will gain dominance over any being. Whole galaxies could be held in thrall unto the awful power of this mighty jewel. And Valkyr, even Valkyr the Hero and Champion of the Gods, was tempted by the power that lay in his hands.

"The Hero God was reluctant to destroy the Demon's Heart, although from their hidden realm the Gods thundered their commands upon him that he do so, and roared in fury until the stars were shaken in their places and the planets trembled. For it seemed unto Valkyr that the jewel was a weapon of such supernal power that it would be dangerous to destroy it... who could say but that in the vastness of Time To Come another such foe might come from the dark abyss to challenge the domain of the Gods? In such a case, the Heart could be used and much battle saved, and many worlds might live on that elsewise would be demolished in the cataclysms of the battle.

"So Valkyr caused to be created on a wilderness world lost in the depths of space a Tower of Iron. Therein he sealed away the Heart of Kom Yazoth forever. A thousand traps and tricks of illusion and divine magic he set to guard the Heart. The secrets of the Tower he kept unto himself alone, nor would he tell of them even to the Gods.

"Mighty beyond telling was the fury of the Gods who rule all the Universes at what they deemed the rebellion of Valkyr. No punishment which their mighty minds could conceive seemed great enough wherewith to repay his revolt against them. But one of them, Zargon the Lord of Punishment and Reward, decreed that for this crime Valkyr must lose his divinity. His life-force, being immortal, they could not destroy, for the Gods exist from eternity to eternity and never taste the black cold wine of death. But they could withdraw from Valkyr his divine status and submerge him in the young races that had arisen upon the planets of the Universe, not nurtured into being by the Children of the Fire Mist. Thus was it done, and the soul of Valkyr went into eternal imprisonment, to live through ten million human lives until it was deemed that he had expiated his crime. But of the Banished God we speak not. We speak of the Heart.

"For the Heart of Kom Yazoth is none other than the Medusa. The jewelled thing that has lain hidden in the Iron Tower since the beginning of time is the frozen crystal heart of the Insatiable One. Its power has not dimmed to this day. He who holds the Medusa can seize control over all the star worlds. Empires themselves cannot stand before the single man who holds the Medusa. The silver-clad legions of invulnerable Valdamar will fall before the awful power of the Medusa. This is the mighty thing of power beyond limit or belief, for which three worlds contend. Which world will triumph, Kirin of Tellus? Pelizon or Zangrimar or Trevelon? Only you can say, for to steal the Heart of Kom Yazoth from the Iron Tower is a task of which only you are worthy…"

Her voice rose, maddening and seductive, filled with allurement and witchery. His heartbeat rose to her winged words.

"If you will abandon the grey mages of Trevelon and ride with me, Kirin of Tellus, I will make you a lord over a thousand suns! No empire in all the past ages of the Universe shall be so mighty as yours. Under my banners you will lead armadas of conquest such as the Universe has never seen before, unconquerable navies of space which shall sweep down upon a thousand worlds, armed with the unconquerable power of the Demon's Heart! I swear to you that you shall stand at my side, beside my Throne of Stars, and we shall rule the Universe together, and together we shall challenge even the eternal Gods themselves! What say you, Kirin—Lord Kirin—Lord of a Thousand Suns!"

A terrible hunger rose within him, a lust such as he had never endured before. It clamored at the gates of his being, thundered against the very citadel of his reason. His will swayed before it, and within his inmost heart, he thrilled to the wild glory of the Witch Queen's challenge…

He had stolen much, dared much, in his dark career, gems had he torn from crown and idol's brow, but never such a theft as this had he dared dream of even in his most grim and fearful dreams!

To steal the heart of a demon! The lure of it shook him. The temptation of such power overwhelmed him, drowned him, beat him down.

How could a mortal, a mere man, resist where even the eternal Gods had fallen beneath the lure of this temptation ere now?

Something moved, deep within him. Like a long-silent part of his mind, stirring to life. Never had he dreamed of crowns and kingdoms; ever before this he had lived for the thrill of adventure, the mystery of danger, the sheer intoxication of standing on the brink of Death's black and yawning door, and laughing, mocking, casting his challenge against that dim portal.

He did not answer. But he knew what he must do.

CHAPTER 7

CAOLA

Temujin was alarmed and somewhat distressed when Kirin did not return to the sphinx-lined hall by the end of the feast. The robot warriors escorted him back to the palatial cell he had shared with the thief and locked him in alone.

He paced the marble floor wearily, his mind busy with troublous thoughts. Although he had eaten (and drunk) hugely, he could not compose himself for sleep, for although he was weary his brain buzzed with nagging worries. He was quite aware of the fascination of the Witch Queen and had seen how Kirin reacted to her allure. As yet, the fat little thaumaturge did not know whether or not the Witch Queen of Zangrimar was also after the Medusa. He thought it very probable, but had no evidence. The mere possibility was hair-raising to contemplate. If that green-faced hussy entraps the lad in her seductive webs, he thought anxiously, there goes Trevelon's hopes out the airlock! There, too, went all dreams of rehabilitating himself in the eyes of his Superiors...

All in all, from whichever direction you examined the possibility, it was dire and dreadful to contemplate.

He began to wish his fondness for the bottle had not come to the attentions of the frosty-hearted Elder Brethren of Trevelon. If he had been a trifle more discreet, or a wee bit more temperate, he might at this hour be snuggled among the plump cushions of his comfortable little room in the monastery, swigging happily from a fat jug of vintage plum brandy, toasting his toes before a sizzling fire, while the wintry winds of ice-bound Trevelon howled impotently beyond the thick stone walls…

Instead, he was stuck in this cursed place, disarmed of his Wand and locked away behind grim ranks of towering steel automata, on an unknown world many light-years from where he wanted to be! It was a doleful predicament. A lamentable set of circumstances. And it was not fair—!

Suddenly the door opened and the little thaumaturge spun around, hoping to see Kirin back safe and sound. Instead it was the slave girl, Caola, with a tray.

"Take it away, my lass; I couldn't eat a thing!" he wheezed in a woebegotten tone, squinting shut his eyes against the tantalizing rotundity of the squat wine-bottle that adorned the tray. The girl said nothing, depositing the tray on a low black table. Then, straightening, she looked around.

"Where is the tall one, your companion?" she inquired. He shrugged with a loud sigh.

"I know not! That green-faced witch lured him away during the feast, and by its ending he had not returned," he said.

The girl came over quickly to where he sat, slumped on the end of a couch.

"Listen to me," she said in a low voice. "I know the reason for which she wishes to win the heart of your friend, the tall one…"

"Kirin."

"Kirin. And she must not succeed!" The vehemence in her voice stung old Temujin from his apathy.

"Whose side are you on, girl?" he demanded.

"Nobody's," she said fiercely. "But I am against her, and her vile schemes. I could not talk before, in fear that she might be listening, for these cells are under surveillance through hidden eyes and ears, but if she is busied using her allure on the tall one, Kirin, she will have no time to eavesdrop on us! I brought the tray only as a pretence. I needed some excuse for getting in to see you…"

"I wondered about that," he chuckled. "Since I had just come from a real feast, a tray of snacks seemed almost like too much hospitality—"

She smiled, her fair cheeks dimpling roguishly.

"Yes, of course! But the metal men who guard the door know nothing of human eating habits and have only rudimentary intelligence at best. They saw me bring a tray in earlier, and I thought they might open to me again …"

"But what is this all about, lass? Why are you involved?"

She shrugged. "I am not native to this world. I am from Nar, the Planet of the Amazons. My ship was forced down just as yours was. She needs recruits, for her plans are to invade the Inner Worlds and topple the young Empire of Valdamar. I care nought for Valdamar, but I am a War Maid, and we are a proud lot as you may have heard. I determined to do everything I could to frustrate her plans in retaliation for my enslavement."

"Good!" he puffed, nodding approvingly.

"That was before I had been in the palace long enough to learn the full measure of her infamy! Listen…"

And in terse, clipped fashion, Caola of Nar recounted the full story of the Medusa, in a narrative substantially the same as the story Azeera had earlier told to Kirin. She left nothing out: the coming of the Transcosmic One into this Universe, the war of the Gods against Kom Yazoth, Valkyr's conquest of the Demon from Beyond and his demolishment of its physical substance—all but the precious

Heart, even the building of the Iron Tower and the Witch Queen's plans to employ the magic power of the Medusa against the star worlds. Temujin was flabbergasted, for he had not until this moment ever heard the full story of the treasure the Iron Tower of Pelizon guarded. Although he had with wink and sly nod suggested to Kirin—without ever really saying it in so many words—that he was in possession of the secret, the plain fact of the matter was that his distrustful Superiors on Trevelon had not told him anything beyond the simplest facts he needed to know in order to carry out his mission.

Now he was utterly appalled at the magnitude of this mission, seeing it in its full importance, and terrified at the thought of how abysmally he had permitted the endeavor to lapse into failure…

"At first I determined I should encumber the Witch Queen for little more than stubbornness," Caola confessed with a small smile. "Then, when I realized the full implications of her plot, I knew I must oppose her for motives more altruistic. She is an evil creature. She must never be permitted to gain power over innocent worlds. We must foil her plans somehow, old one, you and I… and Kirin."

The doctor nodded.

"I agree, lass," he wheezed. "But how? What's the first step? Can you get me out of this cell? Can you find the ivory rod the metal men took from me when we were captured?"

She nodded and drew the slim wand from under the large flat tray she had carried into the room.

"I have it here," she said.

Temujin stifled a glad cry and looked it over anxiously.

"It seems to be in working order," he puffed, "although you can never be certain with the miniaturized devices of the Ancients. Now, can you get me out of here?"

She shook her head.

"Not so fast. I think the first step would be to find out what happened to your friend, Kirin," she said.

"How can you do that?"

"I don't know, but I must try. As a palace slave, I can come and go with considerable freedom here within the building. The metal guards recognize me as one of the slaves and take no notice. The humans—" and here her generous scarlet mouth twisted into an ugly grimace "—those who have gone over to her side, and fawn on her, so as to enjoy titled positions of power in the empire she plans to build, they also take no notice of my comings and goings, as the doings of a slave are beneath the notice of the masters. If they see me in the corridors, they simply assume I am going about some legitimate errand or other, and hence promptly dismiss me from mind." A mocking laugh escaped her. "That is precisely how I learned the legend of Kom Yazoth and found out the plans of the Witch Queen in the first place, by being in places where I had no business and by keeping my ears and eyes open at all times! Fear not, I shall find the Earthling, wherever he is, although it may take a little time…"

With a small smile and wave of her hand, the girl was gone and Temujin was alone again. But not as lonely as before. For now he had an ally. Remembering the strong, vibrant words the girl had spoken and the glint of stubborn determination in her eyes, Temujin relaxed a trifle. Somehow, all did not yet seem lost. Perhaps they had a chance after all…

* * * *

Caola returned to the slave quarters upon leaving the room in which Doctor Temujin and the Earthling, Kirin, had been imprisoned. She mingled with the other slaves, dropping a question here and there, to see if any of her friends had noticed the Earthman or had any idea of his present whereabouts. But none of the other slaves had seen or heard of him since he had been taken from the feasting hall by Azeera several hours ago.

The girl determined she would simply have to set out and find him. And this she promptly did.

She could not disguise, even to herself, a slight personal motive in her anxiety over the tall Earthman. She had conceived an instant attraction for him the first time she saw him, hours before. And, unless she was very much mistaken—and women are hardly ever mistaken in such matters—she believed he felt attracted to her. Remembering the frank admiration in his eyes when he had looked her up and down, she flushed faintly and felt a stirring of excitement.

Caola was a War Maid of Nar. The Amazons of her planet were women warriors. They loved but once in their warlike lives, and that once was forever. And when they gave their love it was to a male stalwart, manly enough to conquer them. Caola was too young to have ever engaged in the War Games that were a gentle euphemism for mating competitions. But she was all woman and deep within her, she longed to be conquered.

The men she had met here on Zangrimar were, in the main, a shallow and sorry lot. Men usually are when they are in subjugation to a woman ruler, and the Zangrimarians were no exception to this rule. They were either cold-hearted, unscrupulous men of avarice and devouring ambition, or languid fops and limp-wristed courtiers, fawners, hangers-on. She loathed them all.

But Kirin was something different. Tall and strong and courageous. His ironic, mocking air, she somehow knew, was an affectation. She longed to know him better, to test his manhood, to fight by his side.

So as she wandered unobtrusively through the wandering ways of the giant citadel, ever on the alert for some token of his presence, she felt her pulses quicken in a very feminine manner at the very thought of his nearness…

* * * *

She very soon exhausted all the more likely places in which Kirin might have been found. The first place was the luxurious suite of apartments reserved for the Witch Queen. Caola dreaded finding him there, in that silken boudoir, perhaps even in the Queen's arms. But the female slaves who resided in the anterooms to these private chambers told her the Queen was not within, and had not returned to her suite since the feast.

A quick tour of the interrogation chambers, the torture rooms, and the high-security cells also produced nothing. And Caola left those grim portions of the palace with a vast sense of relief.

A hunch took her to the apartments of Pangoy, the Queen's confidant and chief advisor. To penetrate here she took extreme cautions not to be seen, for of all the inhabitants of the palace, she feared most the Witch Queen whose sadistic cruelties she had tasted ere now, and secondly the icy-hearted Pangoy, whose cold probing gaze terrified her.

In order to peruse his apartments she employed her intimate knowledge of the ancient structure. She had months ago found a secret passage which meandered between the thick walls of the old fortress. It prowled past many private apartments and contained a secret spy-eye wherethrough the rooms could be examined safely from a place of concealment.

She crept through the dark passage to Pangoy's quarters and utilized the spy-eye. His bedroom was empty; so was his laboratory and sitting room.

But the inner chamber was occupied.

Caola caught her breath sharply. A man's body lay on a metal table, covered by a white cloth. She could not see his face…

This room, she knew, was reserved for Pangoy's strange experiments into the human brain. The Mind Wizard was possessed of certain odd powers, augmented by the telepathic amplifier helmet invented by the terrible savants of his dreaded home-world, Nex.

Here he worked his strange arts upon helpless captives. Here he sought to gain mastery over the minds of others, to bend and crush the wills of former enemies, to force men to become the willing slaves of himself and his mistress, the Witch Queen.

From her position, Caola could not see who lay on the metal table. A great white light blazed down on that table. Straps of pliable metal bound the seemingly unconscious, or dead, figure to the table.

She resolved that she must ascertain the identity of Pangoy's latest victim. Her fingers fumbled along the inner wall of the secret passage, and tripped a catch. A concealed door swung open soundlessly. The girl stepped out into the room.

She went swiftly and silently over to the operating table and reached out for the edge of the cloth that covered the body. But before she could touch it a cold voice rang out harshly behind her—

"What are you doing in this room, girl?"

She turned and looked straight into the chill menace of Pangoy's gaze.

CHAPTER 8

THE MIND PROBE

Before Kirin could phrase his reply to Azeera's offer, a diversion occurred.

"Beware of the Earthling, my lady! He means to betray you."

The cold harsh voice rang out through the stillness of the vaulted room wherein the Space Mirror hung like a globe of mystery above the glistening floor.

Kirin turned to see the man who had entered the chamber unseen by either of them. He was tall and gaunt, with shaven skull. His saffron skin was stretched tightly over sharp cheekbones and jaw, and seamed with a thousand minute, almost invisible wrinkles. His eyes were suave, cool, dark, and appraising. They shone with a mingled amusement and scorn as they probed deep into Kirin's gaze.

Kirin remembered having seen him at the feast, but he had been seated across the hall and they had exchanged no words. Who was the strange man in the purple robe, and—a chill struck through Kirin as the realization hit him—how did he know the direction of Kirin's own inmost thoughts?

Azeera turned to observe the intruder.

"What do you here, Pangoy? Do you dare to spy upon your Queen?" she demanded wrathfully. Scorn flashed in his somber eyes as he shook his head.

"Not on you, my lady, but upon the Earthling, yes. I was determined to observe him during your conversation, while remaining unobserved myself. You know my abilities, hence believe me when I say the Earthling is not to be trusted. He means to acquiesce, but only seemingly. To go along with your plans only on the surface. Actually, he means to steal the Medusa and use it for his own ends."

A cold wave of alarm passed through Kirin, but he fought to control his features and appear calm. "You know my abilities," the gaunt man with cold, suave eyes had purred. Kirin looked him over speculatively. He had seen a man very much like this many years before. The same saffron skin, shaven pate, and cold merciless eyes.

The sense of alarm grew stronger suddenly. Kirin recalled that the other had been a Nexian. Only too well did he know the strange tales men whispered about the ominous and curious powers of the men of Nex. The Mind Wizards of Nex, he mentally corrected himself. This man was a natural telepath!

Cold eyes fastened on his own, Pangoy smiled a cool, enigmatic smile of ironic malice.

"Your musings are correct, dog of Tellus," he purred. "I can indeed read the current of your unspoken thoughts."

Kirin turned to the Witch Queen who surveyed him in silence, the gem-fires of her almond eyes flickering with chill and deadly inquiry. On impulse he blurted out, "He lies, my lady! I say he lies! I know not for what reason, whether to willingly deceive you, or simply because he mis-reads my thoughts, but I say he lies."

His words hung there echoing in the silence of the room. For a time no one spoke. Pangoy stood aloof and disdainful across the chamber, cold mockery in his eyes, a small ironic smile upon his lips, hands tucked into the voluminous sleeves of his purple robe. The Queen stood between them, slender and regal, her jade arms and shoulders rising from the glittering silver sheath of her metallic gown.

"Perhaps," she said softly. "Perhaps he does lie."

A sudden dew glistened on the saffron brows of Pangoy. His smile slipped, faltered, fell. The sheen of perspiration daubed his polished brow.

"My lady, I swear by the thousand gods of space my words are true!"

"Don't believe him, Azeera," Kirin said levelly. "He is trying to deceive you for some unknown purpose of his own."

Her eyes danced with mockery as they turned from Kirin to Pangoy and back again to the dark face of the tall Earthling.

"I am no Mind Wizard, and hence cannot read the inward thoughts of men," she said. "Thus I cannot say which of you two speaks the truth and which utters a vile lie. But I have known Pangoy the longer of you both, and have trusted him ere now. However, I know that he hungers for my love, and is envious of you, Earthling. The jealousy of thwarted lust has often turned a true friend into a deceiving traitor."

Fury writhed across Pangoy's pale, drawn features.

"Never would I by word or deed betray you, my Queen!" he swore in a shaking voice. "I have not earned such scathing words of doubt as these!"

She raised one slim hand to silence him.

"Permit me to finish. I was about to propose a testing of the Earthling." Her eyes glinted with malice and mockery as they burned into Kirin's. "If he speaks the truth and Pangoy lies, we shall easily learn this. Place the Earthling under the Mind Probe!"

From nowhere appeared two of the metal colossi. Grim and expressionless metal masks glared down at him with eyes of red flame as they seized Kirin's arms in their cold grasp and forced him out of the chamber. Pangoy and Azeera followed behind him.

Kirin tried to keep his face impassive, but dismay was in his heart. He had heard of the Mind Wizards of Nex and he knew how they could strip a man's brain bare before the terror of the Probe. He had gambled all on a woman's vanity, hoping to hurl suspicion on Pangoy through the sheer vehemence of his accusation, and because a woman as gorgeous as Azeera would have a natural tendency to believe such an accusation because flattery of her beauty was involved therein.

But he had no illusions. He could not maintain his imposture beneath the merciless beam of the Probe. Before the mental wizardry of the adepts of Nex, his grim determination to stay silent would not long shield him.

Without speaking, he permitted the robot warriors to lead him out of the chamber of the Space Mirror and down a long corridor of glimmering lights.

* * * *

Pangoy and the Witch Queen looked down at the nude figure strapped to the operating table in Pangoy's secret chambers. The Earthling lived, but his respiration was shallow. Sweat glistened on his dark skin and stood in cold globules in the lines of his tortured face. His features were distorted, twisted into a mask of silent agony.

Pangoy felt a certain cold pleasure in stripping the mind of the bold young thief who had thought to steal his own place beside Azeera. A curious helmet now surmounted the brows of the Mind Wizard. It was a domed and glittering thing of metal and crystal. Small odd lights flickered and wove amidst the miniscule mechanisms of the helm. This cunning device acted as an amplifier, to augment and direct the force of Pangoy's own trained mind. To focus his mental probe into a narrow needle-beam with which he searched the shadowy terrain of Kirin's helpless brain like a cartographer reading a map.

Pangoy had not expected a slightest degree of difficulty in laying Kirin's inmost thoughts bare. Only a trained telepath of enormous skill and a vast reservoir of inner power could have hoped to avoid the tremendously magnified strength of Pangoy's brilliant intellect. And, in point of fact, it had been child's play to insinuate a mental tendril through a small crack in the Earthling's mental defenses. The next step had been to intensify pressure against this small flaw until the outer walls of Kirin's mental defenses broke and were crushed. The amplified intelligence of Pangoy could then at his leisure pick through the ruins and expose hidden things to the light of his probing sensors.

But his plans had gone awry.

Just as the mental walls were crumbling and Kirin howled, writhing in the agony of defilement and mental violation, his struggling, tenacious, battling mind somehow tapped a hidden source of mind power. Pangoy knew that the resources of a mind at bay were sometimes extraordinary. But those which Kirin's mind displayed were something beyond the limits of even the Mind Wizard's experience.

What had happened was swift and inexplicable. One moment the naked Earthling panted and fought against the Probe, the next instant he was plunged into a death-like sleep. In this trance-like state his mind was dead, lax, unreadable. All energy seemed to drain instantly from the memory-sequences. To the telepathic vision of Pangoy, these mental chains were like glowing paths that coiled and twisted between and around the dim glowing nuclei of the instinctive mind-centers. The blazing memory-sequences could be read like so many illuminated signs. But suddenly the energy source was annulled. The glowing sequences died into somnolent darkness. In the death-like darkness of Kirin's mind, Pangoy's attempts to probe his thoughts were useless.

Feeling an unaccustomed sense of frustration, Pangoy one by one withdrew his mind tendrils from the dead citadel. The lights in the steel and crystal helm dimmed, went out. Wearily he removed the curious headpiece and set it in its place atop a low pedestal.

This unusual mental defense-mechanism was something completely beyond Pangoy's experience. He could do nothing further until such time as the Earthling awakened from his unnatural and death-like trance. He sought to explain this to the Witch Queen.

"I had hoped to strip his mental defenses to such a stage that you could question him yourself, my lady. In such a condition his conscious mind would be helpless and the answers to your queries would spring automatically from his memory-circuits. It is impossible for a man to lie under the Probe; hence you would learn the truth of his accusations and the falsehood of his counter-claims…"

She raised a hand for silence.

"Enough, Pangoy! I am not fully satisfied in the truth of your statements. Let me warn you that if you have slain the Earthling under guise of preparing him for my questioning, if you have destroyed his mind to protect your own position, my vengeance shall be sudden and terrible."

He bowed humbly before the icy scorn in her voice.

"I swear to you that he lives and is sane! This trance condition is beyond my knowledge, but he will recover normal consciousness with time. Then we shall continue the Probe and you can discover for yourself whether I speak the truth or whether I lie…"

"Very well, Pangoy. We shall continue this at a later time," she said, and together they left the laboratory.

* * * *

Kirin was fully conscious of everything about him as Pangoy and Azeera discussed his condition. Although he could hear perfectly his eyes were closed and he had no knowledge of where he was. And he was unable to lift his eyelids and look. It was as if an unbreakable paralysis seized control of all his faculties. Although he strove desperately to break the spell that bound him as if with invisible chains, he could not so much as move a muscle.

His lungs expanded. His chest rose and fell. His heart pumped red blood through his body. All automatic life systems continued operation. But every conscious ability was numbed and rendered helpless. It was an eerie and terrifying state; it was as if his mind was a prisoner, locked and helpless within his own skull.

Within his mind strange forces were at work. He was conscious of them but in a vague, dim way. It was as if doors long sealed were opening one by one. Strange hulking shapes arose from the dark sediment of his bottomless unconscious. Whole unknown segments of memory rose slowly from the black well of the lower mind, that enormous reservoir of racial memory where the conscious mind can never trespass.

The sensation was uncanny. As if colossal submerged icebergs were lifting their titanic bulk out of an unknown and shadowy sea. Enormous sequences of memory rose slowly into the light of his upper mind and connected to his memory circuits. He caught glimpses of unknown lands, strange faces, curious symbols. Colors unknown to mortal man flashed before the inward eye of his mind. Tumbling panoramas of fantastic beauty, strangeness and terror rose into view.

There were colossal mountains of blazing crystal that covered the surface of an unknown planet. Titanic storms of flying fire clove and shattered the crystal ranges and brought their glittering escarpments down in a rain of ringing shards.

Other sectors of previously-submerged memory rose into place, linking with yet more, forming a colossal pattern. It was like the pieces of a mental jigsaw puzzle coming together into a whole.

There were vast and unfamiliar winged shapes of fierce light hurtling through regions of golden coiling mist towards an unknown goal. Then surging mists drove these things from view and when they parted he stared down on the strange purple waters of a nameless sea. Here a scaled and finny folk dwelt in coral cities adorned with giant pearls. He saw their glittering silvery bodies as they clove the winy foam. He watched as they tamed gigantic monsters of the depths to serve as their steeds and as animate weapons of war in a colossal conflict with feathery avians who dwelt in cloud realms above the surface. The wars of the sea and air seemed to occupy endless centuries of slow time. At length the mists drove all from view again.

He was conscious of remembering the sensation of rapid flight through regions of utter darkness and terrible cold. Then the darkness fell away and he strode through halls of golden splendor, where tall faceless beings were throned amidst thunderous light. He stood before them.

Streams of unintelligible converse flowed about him; vaguely he understood that a mighty task had been set upon him, a quest of some nature beyond his powers of comprehension.

He departed helmed and armed and cloaked with terrific forces. He descended through seas of stars to a miniature spiral of light, a jewelled pinwheel that looked like a glittering toy against the dark of the abyss. With a distinct shock, the portion of Kirin's mind that observed these dim memories recognized that jewelled spiral as the galaxy wherein he had been born.

There a Thing moved across the stars. It was invisible; to the sight it could be glimpsed only as a clotted thickness of shadows, a greater darkness against the dark. He closed in battle with the crawling blot of darkness. Tremendous forces surged in that titanic conflict. Stars were torn flaming from their place and hurled against the coiling gloom. Streams of enthropy were levelled against it that would have withered into nothingness any material being. Naught availed against the Thing, ever it came on across starry space.

At length he closed with it in something akin to hand-to-hand battle. Coils of silken shadows settled about him. A wintry cold blew from the clotted nest of writhing night. He battled with blasts of heat and searing light. And then...

But the mind of Kirin was not able to handle the flood of intolerable memories that rose from the dark gulf within his deeper brain. He sank into astounded, stunned unconsciousness. One name, one strange and curious name, echoed and resounded through the vaults of his memory.

Somewhere he had heard that name before, but the sound of it conveyed no meaning to his over-loaded brain.

Valkyr... Valkyr... I am Valkyr!

He sank into the darkness of deep slumber.

And while he slept, the hidden Second Mind that had shared this body with him all his life, rose into wakefulness and into realization of itself. The probing tendrils of the Mind Wizard had triggered an automatic protective reaction. A slumbering intelligence long dormant was roused to wakefulness again by the threat of mental violation. As Kirin slept this intelligence swiftly reorganized itself, linked memory sectors together into patterns of supernal power, and began at leisure to explore the surface recordings of recent events. For millions of years the dead and banished God had endured incarnation after incarnation in mortal form. When one host-body died, the disembodied intelligence fled from the corpse to enter another life. Now was it reborn within Kirin of Tellus.

Knowing none of this, the Earthling slept, until awakened by a girl's shrill scream of terror!

CHAPTER 9

MIND DUEL

"I ask you once again, slave—what are you doing in my quarters?"

The menace in Pangoy's voice was sharp and cold, like a keen dagger-blade.

Caola turned, wishing she had brought some manner of weapon. Fear rose within her. She knew the dire things of which the vile Nexian was capable, and she knew that the life of a slave-girl was of no consequence on Zangrimar, under the tyrannical reign of the Witch Queen.

"Lord, I—I—" she stammered, her mind racing furiously.

"You what? You came here to spy, is that it?"

"No! I came only to…"

He sprang forward and seized her wrist, twisting it in a merciless grip.

"Speak, girl, or I will break your arm," Pangoy hissed, exerting subtle pressure. "Whom are you spying for? What faction? Is it Kynarion, or Loigar, or Iosophus, or—the Queen? Speak, you little fool!"

Sobbing with pain, Caola writhed in the Nexian's terrible grip. Her arm blazed with agony. Needles of intolerable fire lanced through her muscles.

"Please, Lord Pangoy! I spy for no one. I am here by accident—a wrong turning of the corridor—" He smiled mirthlessly.

"You lie, girl. My chambers are clearly marked. You would have to be blind to enter here by error. And the door is sealed by magic, it opens only to the touch of the signet ring I wear. Speak the truth now, or I'll—"

He increased the pressure and Caola screamed.

It was this shrill cry that woke Kirin from his slumbers. He opened bleared eyes to see the girl struggling in the clutches of Pangoy. Although every movement cost him pain, he fought against the straps that held him.

"Caola! Let her go, you torturing fiend!"

Pangoy cast a look of astonishment at the man he had thought incapacitated for hours. Then he smiled and hurled the whimpering girl against the wall with one powerful shove.

"So, we have awakened from our little swoon, eh? How nice!" he chuckled, striding towards the table whereon Kirin writhed helplessly.

"Don't touch her again, you pig, or I'll break both of your arms," Kirin growled.

Pangoy smiled again.

"So that's it! You have a friend within the palace, eh? This girl did not enter my quarters by accident, but to discover where you were hidden... I see! A conspiracy. How many others are in this, girl? Speak up!"

He turned away from the bound Earthling to confront the slave-girl who had staggered to her feet. One hand went to his waist where the glittering metal coil of a neuronic whip dangled.

Caola sucked in her breath when she saw it. She had seen slaves in agony under the neuronic whip before and she knew the incredible agony the touch of the electric lash caused. The metal of the whip was charged with electric force keyed to the vibrations of the human nervous system. A single touch brought a burst of unendurable agony searing through every nerve in the body. She moaned and lifted her hands in mute supplication as Pangoy drew forth the whip.

Bound to the table, Kirin also saw and recognized the whip. The girl he fuzzily remembered had been friendly to himself and Doctor Temujin in their cell, hours or days before. Although his mind throbbed with red waves of pain and his body felt like it had been beaten with clubs on every square inch, he strove against the metal straps. And they shattered!

The squeal of rending metal screeched through the chamber. Pangoy jerked around, his face blank with amazement, to behold the Earthling's nude body descending from the table. Those straps should have held a bull buphodon helpless. But they had shattered into atoms beneath one surge of the Earthling's muscles!

He raised the whip against Kirin as the Earthling stumbled towards him. The power-pack in the hilt of the whip sparked with energy as Pangoy thumbed the power switch. Blue flickering flames wavered along the length of the lashing metal whip. The pungence of ozone filled the chamber.

Pangoy shook out the neuronic whip. Fiery sparks spat and crackled.

"Kirin, look out!" Caola cried. But the Earthling lurched forward, unheeding. Some nameless force rose within his mind, directing his steps. He was caught in the grip of an unseen master and sent staggering forward like a jointed puppet guided by an invisible hand.

Pangoy laughed and lashed out with the whip.

Kirin reached up and caught it. Fire sizzled about his arm, but unseen webs of force turned aside the electric flames before they could touch and sear his flesh. Force webs bent and the very fabric of space twisted. Energy was turned back upon its own source.

And the whip-handle exploded in Pangoy's hand!

With a deafening retort the power-pack in the handle detonated. There was a fierce flash of white fire and the Mind Wizard recoiled, shrieking, clutching his burnt and blackened hand. Minute droplets of super-heated liquid metal sizzled, deeply imbedded in his seared flesh.

Caola watched, her eyes widening with incredulity, as Kirin advanced step by step upon the crippled Mind Wizard. Pangoy awoke to the danger that confronted him and turned from the Earthling's path, hurrying over to the laboratory bench. There he snatched up the mind-amplifying helmet and set it upon his brows. His features were pale with agony and contorted with rage and baffled fury.

Never in the seven centuries of his surgically-prolonged existence had Pangoy of Nex been so outrageously treated. He lusted for revenge. Now, with the invincible mind helmet at his command, he could hold off a hundred warriors. Lights flashed into being amidst the sparkling coils of glass and metal that adorned the curiously-shapen helm.

He hurled a mental bolt at the naked Earthling.

The bolt of mind force was immaterial, but it struck like the blow of a sledge-hammer, thudding into Kirin's belly. Breath gusted from his lungs. He sagged and fell forward to his knees, gasping with intolerable pain. The mental bolt had struck at those nerve-centers of the brain that registered pain. They stimulated the nerve-sequences connected to the Earthling's solar plexus. The result was the exact neural simulation of a body blow of terrific force; there was no way of determining a genuine blow from a neurally-simulated one, since the nerve centers of Kirin's brain could only register the pain caused.

As he sagged on his knees, gasping for breath, a lash of liquid fire seared his bent back. He stiffened erect under the fiery touch. Then a terrific blow to one temple sent him sprawling, his mind be-fogged. He clung to consciousness with tenacity, enduring the buffets that tore and flailed at his defenseless body. A red whirling mist arose to engulf his mind. He was moments from unconsciousness.

Then a surge of extraordinary vitality ran through him. It was as if in the last extremity of his endurance, he had tapped some hidden source of inner strength. Slowly, stiffly, incredibly, he rose to his feet, ignoring the whirling storm of invisible blows that lashed his flesh.

Pangoy gaped incredulously. Brows knotted in fury, he redoubled the frenzied attack.

But Kirin felt nothing. Invisible force ran throughout his body. Nerve centers were insulated against the simulated attacks of the mental bolts. The bolts were deflected. Kirin towered indomitable and victorious; the Mind Wizard was helpless to cause him harm.

Then the tide of battle turned. From somewhere, Kirin became aware of a weird extension of himself. He struck out with it and watched the Mind Wizard stagger back, reeling under a hail of invisible blows. It was an uncanny experience. Kirin had become aware of his brain as if it were an extra limb he had never used till now. Suddenly he knew precisely how to strike out with the power of his mind alone, how to hurl irresistible force into the brain of his opponent. Surging power drove from him. Bolts of mental fury slammed Pangoy against the wall. The helmet fell from his nodding brows and exploded in mid-air.

Kirin mentally plucked up the half-conscious Wizard and sent his helpless body crashing into the lab table. It went over in a cascade of shattering glass and splattering fluids. Chemicals mixed together, smoldering into flame. A spray of liquid fire splashed over the unconscious body of Pangoy. His torn robes ignited in a soundless flash. In a second he was sheathed in a chrysalis of blinding white fire.

Swaying numb and half-conscious amidst the shambles, Kirin suddenly came to himself again. His mysterious mastery of mental power vanished as inexplicably as it had come. Nerves no longer sustained against sensation now shrieked with pain. He felt numb, bruised, pummeled. He staggered and would have fallen amidst the running pools of flaming fluids, but Caola caught his arm and steadied him. He blinked through oily chemical smoke to peer at her tear-stained face.

"What happened?" he mumbled.

"I… don't know," she said faintly. "You fought Pangoy and… you conquered him!"

"Where is he?"

She tugged at his arm. "He is dead. Quick! We have little time to waste. The fire will be noticed. The alarm will be given and the metal men will come. Quick—here are your garments."

With the help of the War Maid, Kirin struggled into his suit of grey celloflex, seamed it up, and followed her into the black opening that led to the secret passage through the walls of the citadel.

The door swung shut behind them on a scene of flaming wreckage amidst which the blacked corpse of Pangoy the Nexian lay staring mindlessly, contemplating nothingness.

CHAPTER 10

STEEL AGAINST STEEL!

Within the secret passage, Caola led Kirin through unbroken darkness. The sudden surge of amazing strength
wherewith the Earthling had battled against the mental
forces of Pangoy had now ended, and he was drained
of energy. His skull throbbed with red waves of pain; it
rung like a beaten anvil. His arms and legs were numbed,
drained of strength. Several times he stumbled and would
have fallen had it not been for the quick-minded girl at his
side, who supported him with strong arms. There was no
time to rest. They must go forward.

The walls of the passage were thin. They could hear
the banshee-scream of alarms, the ringing feet of steel
warriors as they gathered to quench the fires that had
turned the ruined laboratory of Pangoy into a blinding in-
ferno. Obviously, the corridor beyond was thronged with
their enemies. They could not yet emerge from the hidden
passage concealed behind the walls. Caola did not know
what to do.

She had explored much of the network of secret spy-
ways that wound through the ancient citadel, but she was
familiar only with a portion of them. She feared to go too
far beyond her accustomed paths, lest they become lost in
the maze of hidden passages. The only alternative was to
sit here in the close darkness and wait for the halls to be
cleared so they could come out through one of the secret
doors, and that course would lose them their single slim
advantage: time.

Half-fainting, Kirin slumped at her side, gasping for breath, knuckling his aching brows in dumb agony. He had suffered excruciatingly under the torments of the Mind Probe, and his body had taken an unmerciful pummeling during his battle with the Nexian. He was in no condition to think clearly or to fight. To risk the corridors would be foolhardy.

"Why are we… just standing here?" he mumbled. The girl explained their predicament in brief words. He rubbed his temples, striving to use his wits.

"Do these passages… extend into the cells where… Doc and I were kept?"

"I do not know," she confessed hesitantly. "I have never had reason to find out. Mostly, I have used the secret passages in the central part of the palace, to spy on the Witch Queen and her councils…"

"Well, now is as good a time as any," he grunted. "Let's see if they do."

So they went forward in the pitch-darkness of the passages, and Caola desperately hoped her sense of direction would lead her rightly. It was risky to use the spy-eyes when the halls were filled with people, and one corridor looked very much like another. Still, there was nothing to do but try…

* * * *

Doctor Temujin waited, fretful and anxious, for the return of Caola with some word as to the whereabouts and the fate of Kirin. Time seemed to stretch out unendurably. He had no timepiece and hence could not correctly fudge the elapsed interval, but it seemed like long hours since she had left him behind.

Then came a disturbance. The shrill clangor of alarms, the crash of metal feet against the stone-paved stair. The shout of human voices. The tension of not knowing what was happening became unbearable. He gnawed the end of his mustache, wringing his fat hands, groaning at the suspense. For all he knew, Caola might have been captured and her mission revealed... for all he knew, Kirin might be in the corridor beyond, battling hopelessly against the horde of steel-clad titans who guarded this citadel of sorcery...

At last he could wait no longer, he must find out what was happening! Luckily, the slave-girl had brought him his slim ivory rod. He fondled it with loving hands. Not only was the device a powerful weapon, but a cunning tool with many uses.

He made certain adjustments to the controls in the hilt, muttering a potent mantrum under his breath as he did so. Then he reversed the wand so that its pointed end was directed towards his body. He released the power switch concealed in the handle.

A stream of invisible force enveloped him from head to foot. Carefully he turned his body so as to make certain that every part of his anatomy was bathed in the invisible rays that now emanated from the Rod of Power.

Had anyone been in the luxurious cell with him at the time, they would have been astounded at the miraculous change that passed slowly over the fat form of the little thaumaturge. His plump rotundity became ghostly and translucent. Through his limbs and torso an observer could have seen the dim outlines of walls and furniture. Slowly, his body became as transparent as air itself, until at length Temujin was completely invisible.

In this curious and temporary state, he was blinded. To him it seemed as if he stood in utter and unrelieved blackness. This was the natural result of the weird transformation caused by the high-energy rays emitted by his ivory instrument. The rays aligned the molecular structure of his component particles until the magnetic poles of his atoms were mono-directional. No longer did the photons of light rebound from the surface of his body, repelled by contact with the magnetic fields of his atomic structure. Now every atom pointed in a single direction, and the light that touched him passed through his body without hindrance. It was like opening the bunds upon a window: the slats all pointing in the direction of the light-source permit light rays to pass through the shuttered windows. Only the comparatively minute edges of the blinds catch and repel the light. Thus it was with Temujin's body; the alignment of the magnetic poles made his flesh 99.99% invisible.

He padded swiftly to the door and fumbled across it until his fat fingers found the lock. Then he altered the setting of his wand and released a narrow stream of intense energy against the mechanism. Metal fused, glowed white, and flowed down the surface of the door in superheated droplets. He edged the door open slightly and squeezed out. Now he was in the hall. There should have been at least two of the metal robot guards stationed before the portal, but in his blinded condition he could not see them. It was a great drawback in the invisibility process that the retinas of his eyes were also rendered transparent to light under the effect of the ray. Light passed through his eyes without reacting upon the rod-and-cone mechanism of the organs. Alas, there was no help for it. He stood still and listened.

Straining his ears, he heard a high-pitched and almost inaudible burst of electronic "noise." One of the robots was communicating to its companion the fact that the door they guarded was now partially open. He listened for the reply, and when it came he now formed a mental picture of the position of .he two automatons in relation to himself. Hence he stepped lightly around them and tiptoed off down the corridor in the direction of the alarm and clamor.

He sidled along one wall of the corridor, for he could never know when someone might come by, and not being able to see Temujin the stranger might very well collide with him if he were foolish enough to walk through the middle of the hall in his present blinded and invisible state. But few people walk along the far side of a hall, commonly preferring the clear space in the center. Hence, although several persons or automata went past him, none so much as brushed against the fat little wizard.

He came to a junction of two halls. Here, he remembered, a coiling flight of steps led down to a lower level. This was a tricky space to navigate in his blinded condition, but he went carefully, feeling his way with outstretched fingers wherever possible.

The stench of burning cloth and wood came to his nostrils. He heard men coughing and exclaiming. Someone had caused a fire in the further portions of the palace, that was obvious. He wondered if his friends could be the culprits, and if the fire was intended as a diversion.

A dim wavering light became visible.

Temujin froze, convulsed with shock. He knew the effect of the invisibility ray was strictly temporary. He dimly recalled from his studies that it generally lasted at least a half an hour before wearing off. Could he have allowed so much time to pass while he gingerly felt his way along? Or was the time element other than he remembered? He groaned a curse, if only he had paid closer attention to his classes in the Lesser Thaumaturgies!

There was no question about it, he was slowly becoming visible. The shadowy likeness of a huge hall was coming into being about him. He sprinted across the intersection of the corridors in order to gain the fullest possible advantage before coming to full visibility.

Then a harsh iron voice froze him cowering in his tracks. An amplified voice roared and echoed through the palace.

"The magician Temujin is missing from his cell, and the Earthling Kirin has somehow escaped, slaying the Lord Pangoy in his flight! All nobles and slaves are warned to watch for these escaped prisoners. The Earthling is not to be harmed, merely seized; but the magician Temujin is of no use to us and may be armed and dangerous. The fat man is to be shot down on sight, by order of the Queen!"

Temujin moaned an entreaty to several gods and waddled towards a tapestry-hung wall where he might be able to hide. Shot down on sight! Even as he quivered at the deadly flavor of those words, the entire rotunda sprang into full view and he looked down at his fat hands. They were firm and solid to the sight. He was no longer invisible…

And he heard the tramp of metal feet coming up the curving marble stair. He knew he could not reach the further wall in time. But he ran for it anyway…

And slipped and fell sprawling, just as the first robots came up the stair into the rotunda behind him.

* * * *

Caola and Kirin had almost reached the luxurious cell wherein he and Doctor Temujin had been imprisoned hours or days before, when they heard the grim announcement that ran through every chamber of the giant citadel. Kirin's jaw tightened grimly.

"How do you suppose the Doc got out?" he demanded. "Did you tell him about this network of secret passages? Maybe he went looking for one in the cell..."

The girl shook her head, tousling her tawny mane of loose hair. "I don't think I even mentioned them to him," she said. Suddenly she laid her hand on his arm. "What was that?" A hoarse squall of terror had sounded through the thin false wall from the spaces beyond.

"I don't know," he said tensely. "But it sounded like the Doc..."

Risking much, he dared a swift peek through the nearest spy-eye. There was always the danger that someone passing through the hall beyond might catch a glimpse of the lensed opening as it was momentarily visible when the eye was in use.

He looked out and saw the huge rotunda where corridors met and the stairwell ascended to this level. He saw Temujin sprawled in the center of the open area, facing a rank of robot warriors who had just mounted the stairs. He heard the almost-inaudible high-speed squeal of robotic speech and guessed that the lead robot was informing his fellows of the identity of the fat little human sprawled helplessly in their path. Even as he watched, Temujin brought his ivory wand up, pointing it at the commanding robot. The wand spat sizzling lightning! Blue fire snapped. Long hissing sparks crawled over the helmet-like face of the automaton. A muffled explosion thumped. Oily black smoke seethed from the jointures in the robot's armor and the red glare of his vision-lenses died. The metal giant tottered on his feet and fell forward against the marble floor with a terrific crash of jangling metal.

"Let 'em have it, Doc!" Kirin yelled. He thumbed the catch and a secret panel opened in the wall through which he sprang out into the rotunda, racing to the aid of the fat thaumaturge.

Wheezing, Temujin lurched to his feet as the file of robots came clanking down on him. His wand blazed electric fire, shattering the shoulder-joint of the foremost automaton. The metal casing shattered and the limb went flying. The maimed mechanical staggered into a comrade and jostled him from his stance. The metal man, flailing to regain his lost balance, crashed against the balustrade. Thin sculpted marble broke before his weight, hurling him over the edge. He fell to the landing below with a tremendous crash of rending steel.

Although he ached in every nerve and sinew, Kirin hurried to the side of the embattled thaumaturge. The Rod of Power was slow-working and could not hold the massed squadron of steel-clad war-machines at bay for long. And already the alarm was spreading—broadcast by one of the robots, no doubt, using a radio beam to contact the central command post of the palace forces. Again the magnified voice rang out through the citadel.

"The missing prisoners have been located on the Ninth Level, in the White Rotunda at the junction of corridors 9-delta and 11-beta. They are armed with energy weapons and are under attack by guard squadron 104. All units advance to block exits leading to those halls—"

"Good to see you in one piece, lad," Temujin puffed, cocking a merry blue eye at the Earthling. "Sorry about all this fuss, though!"

"Forget it—wish I had my gun. Can you hold 'em off, Doc? Caola is holding the panel open—there's a secret passage in the wall right over there—"

"So that's where you popped from! I was wondering!" Temujin broke off to blast one of the metal men to flying fragments with a bolt directed at the center of its steel thorax.

"Alas, I doubt if I can keep this up much longer," he wheezed. "These rods are not inexhaustible, you know."

"Quickly!" the girl called from the black opening in the wall. "This way—Azeera comes!"

"Let's go, Doc," Kirin snapped. "Back up towards the wall. Keep holding them off with your blast the best you can…"

"Hold, Earthling!"

The cold silver voice froze him in his tracks. He turned and saw a fearful sight. Azeera slowly melted into being out of thin air in the center of the rotunda. By whatever science miracle of the Ancients her materialization was accomplished, it was clearly no illusion. She was present in the flesh and wild with rage.

The cold inhuman beauty of her jade features was distorted into a carven mask of utter fury. Her eyes blazed with hatred. Her jet-black hair had burst loose from her slender coronet and floated about her head like a halo of black flames. The silken gown clung to every sinuous curve of her magnificent body, accentuating the lines of breast and hip and thigh with glittering silver fire.

Gone was the seductress, the alluring siren. This was Azeera, the tyrant queen of Zangrimar, terrible as a mad goddess in her rage, and armed with might. Kirin's heart sank to behold her in her wrath.

As she held him at bay with the blaze of her witchery, he dimly heard the clank of steel-shod legions coming from either hall. They were trapped between three forces, and at the mercy of the Witch Queen. And he had no gun! How could mere mortal flesh do battle against hard steel?

And then, in the utter extremity of his need, that mysterious Other Presence within him woke once more. A tide of more-than-human power surged through his weary, battered body and aching brain. He felt a tingling flood of fresh vigor sweep through every cell and nerve and organ of his body. His mind became crystal clear, sharply focused. From hidden depths within him, that eerie command over mind forces awoke once again... the same force that had against all odds destroyed Pangoy the Nexian earlier. A boundless confidence filled him. How can flesh battle against steel...?

He answered his own unspoken question aloud.

"It can't. But we can set steel against steel... !"

As Temujin and Caola regarded him with puzzled, almost frightened eyes, the Earthling straightened. The bright glory of a God flamed into being around him, like a visible aureole of Power.

He held out his hands against the oncoming horde of steel warriors. And then he struck.

CHAPTER 11

SKY BATTLE

For a moment it seemed as if nothing had happened. Then the advancing line of robots coming down the opposite hall stopped dead. They milled in confusion. The air shrilled with the squeal of electronic conversation as they babbled to one another in strange confusion.

Then the foremost of their number turned on the second and battered in his head!

Circuits shorted with a blaze of sparks. The dead colossus fell sprawling, and his metallic murderer turned to assault a second victim. Caola, Temujin and the Witch Queen stared in awe and astonishment at this unexpected diversion.

The rank of robots on the stair, who had been first to accost the fallen Temujin, now broke the strange paralysis that had halted their progress as well. Steel limbs rose and fell, as metal warriors roared in battle with their former comrades. Stone cracked and splintered as steel gladiators, locked in combat, shattered through the balustrade and fell to the landing below.

Within instants the metal horde were caught in a fury of internecine strife. Ignoring the humans, they fell upon each other in a fury of blind rage. The din of battle was terrific, as steel claws wrenched and tore at steel limbs, as clubbed extremities battered in metal skulls, stove in steel-clad thorax and chest.

Blue fire spat from torn wires. Power centers detonated deafeningly, blasting metal bodies apart. Oily smoke seethed from steaming bodies of the fallen.

Azeera was frozen in astonishment. Never in the long years of her reign had her metal legions revolted against her supremacy. Now it seemed that her robot warriors had gone mad!

"Stop, you fools! I, your Queen, command you to cease!"

The metal-clad horde turned to regard her. Then, stilling their combat, they marched forward again. Kirin—who alone knew what had happened—seized the gaping doctor and jerked him aside, out of the path of the metal giants. They tramped across the rotunda towards the place where Azeera stood. Behind her, at the mouth of the other hall, a similar troop advanced, and up the stairway came a third.

Azeera screamed as realization came to her; terror flamed in her glorious eyes. She clawed at the crystal scepter that danged like an ornate, jewelled toy at her girdle. Lambent green flame welled from its tip. Tendrils of emerald radiance whipped out to writhe about the limbs of the oncoming steel colossi. They fell, some of them, immobilized by the force of her magic weapon. But the others marched forward...

She fell, trampled and torn beneath the steel-shod legs of her mechanical slaves. It was a grim sight to behold ,and Temujin shuddered to see it. Caola paled and turned away. Even Kirin turned aside, his thin lips tightening, his face bleak. He did not look again at the torn and scarlet thing that wriggled feebly beneath the crushing tread of the marching automata...

He knew not how he had done the thing, but he had directed a blast of electric force against the robot horde. Their reasoning centers, overloaded, had gone dead. Mindless, they obeyed only the last order they had received—to kill!

And in their blind fury, they had crushed and trampled down Azeera, the Witch Queen of Zangrimar, into death. She had dreamed of whelming the Inner Worlds beneath her steel-shod legions. Well, the Inner Worlds had naught to fear from her now...

The thunder of conflict when the three files of marching robots encountered each other echoed from the curved walls of the rotunda. In seconds, the air was filled with a frightful din. And from other portions of the palace, Kirin heard a similar uproar. It would seem that the force he had directed against their robot foes had passed through the entire citadel.

Every robot in the palace had gone mad and was attacking anything that moved or lived.

It was a good time to be gone from this scene of carnage. He caught the attention of his comrades, gesturing since he could not be heard above the uproar, pointing to the far end of the rotunda where a balcony opened beyond a line of marble columns.

Avoiding the chaos of battling mechanical men, they went out onto the balcony. Just below, where a landing area jutted out from the wall of the citadel, he spotted an unoccupied sky sled. In a matter of seconds he had helped Temujin and Caola over the balustrade and down to the lower level. He clambered down himself and they ran to the sled. It had been under guard, but the two automatons had turned upon each other, maddened by the deadening of their reasoning centers, and had battered each other into wreckage.

"Quick, let's get out of here," he growled, helping the girl up onto the sled. Puffing, the little thaumaturge scrambled atop the shallow oval platform of the flying machine.

"Onolk, Maryash, and Thaxis of the Spears, lad, what the devil did you do back there?" Temujin wheezed.

"I swear I don't know... something came over me," Kirin said wonderingly.

Suddenly the balcony jumped beneath them, knocking them sprawling. Black webwork splintered through the marble facing of the landing area. Smoke boiled up beyond the castled crest of the citadel above them. All over the visible portion of the citadel, lights went dead.

"That must have been a central power source," he grunted. "Come on, no time to sit and talk now!"

Settling Caola and the little thaumaturge in the low seats that ran around the outer edge of the sky sled, Kirin made his way forward to the control chair. He seated himself before a gleaming crystal pedestal, similar to the one he had watched in use when they had been brought here from the space field. He hoped he could remember how the robot pilot had controlled the craft. He fumbled with searching hands across the surface of the glistening column. Lights flickered into life within the translucent substance. Ah... thus, and so... yes!

"I thought it might come in handy, knowing how to operate one of these things," he laughed. "So I paid attention when we were flown in from the ship. Hold on, now."

Like an autumn leaf caught by an updraft of wind, the twenty-foot-long oval of gleaming plastic swung up from the landing area and drifted up into the air. Wind plucked at Kirin's hair and made his eyes water as he swung the craft out over the city.

It was early evening. Eight or nine moons hung like pallid lanterns in the dusky sky. Lights twinkled along the coiling avenues of the metal metropolis and the tall towers blazed with radiance against the gathering gloom.

Seemingly, the madness of the robots had not spread beyond the confines of the palace, for as they dipped and soared over broad avenues and plazas they could see no sign of chaos or battle.

Kirin wondered if the ship was still bound helpless in the force field that had captured them. Did the ship brain live, or was it still shut off? He activated his wristlet, which was radio-connected to the brain, but got no response. There was no time to pursue the matter, for he suddenly saw a rising wedge of sky sleds similar to the one in which they rode. The other craft rose from the roof of a long low structure beneath, to block their path.

Caola stifled a low cry.

"Look out—we are being intercepted by the Perimeter Patrol," she called.

Kirin nodded grimly. "So I see. And I don't think this craft has any guns. Doc, how's your wand holding out? Still got some juice left?"

Temujin shook his head.

"The charge must be almost exhausted by now, lad. I used it pretty frequently back there, along towards the last. The power cells are self-renewing. They extract energy from cosmic radiation, but the repowering process takes time. At least an hour."

"There goes that idea!" Kirin slitted his eyes against the stinging wind-stream and leaned over the edge to peer down. "We'll have to try dodging them. Hang on tight—"

As the foremost sleds raced towards them, Kirin lifted the craft in a dizzy climb that had the sled almost standing on edge. He stepped up the power and they soared above the advancing patrol. When they reached the two thousand foot level, he leveled off and flew straight towards the distant space field. It lay far across the width of the steel city from here. He knew they would not reach it in time…

The pursuing craft were on their tail, and drawing closer. Even as he caught a swift glance behind, a flash of intense fire blazed from one of the leading craft. White flame exploded in mid-air a little to his left. The concussion rocked their sled violently. He spun about in a half-circle. And came down shrieking to a lower level, beneath the patrol.

Again he straightened out and flew for the field. But the patrol had caught on to his evasive actions and came settling down all around him, bracketing his sled. He could fly no lower for he was skimming the crest of some of the buildings now. And he could not break through the blanketing tactic of the enemy craft to ascend again. His lips tightened grimly. This was the end. The robot warriors would have no difficulty in forcing him down to the ground now.

If only he had a gun! But his hand weapon was left behind in the palace. It had been taken from him when he had been first captured, and he had never seen it again…

The sleds above were settling down almost on top of him now. Forcing him down. He swung swiftly to one side at a sharp angle, hoping to come out from under the blanket of sleds.

But the robots were watchful and had anticipated his next move. The squadron above wheeled and darted in the same direction, moving all at once like a trained phalanx.

"End of the line, I guess," he grunted sourly.

And then the sled on his left came apart in mid-air. Crimson fire flashed blindingly. Bits of hot plastic rattled on the surface of his sled.

"What th—"

And then one on his right exploded. Black smoke whipped past them and was gone.

"Hang on tight," he yelled, and lifted the sled, driving straight up through the hole left by the blasted sled. By some miracle he was up and out of the opening before the rest of the formation had time to block him. Now he was well above them and flying at full velocity. But they were climbing after him... or were they?

He peered down and saw them disintegrate one by one. Fire blossomed briefly as the pursuers exploded, shedding plumes of black hot smoke and showers of molten plastic on the metropolis below.

"What's happening, lad?" Temujin gasped. Kirin shrugged, a joyous grin lighting his face.

"I have no idea, but I hope it keeps up!"

It did. The last of the pursuing craft vanished in flame and thunder, and the sky was theirs.

Or was it?

A dark shape blotted out the skies above. Temujin squawked and pointed.

"By the Beard of Arnam, lad—isn't that your ship?"

Kirin craned his neck and looked. It was indeed! The huge black shape was almost invisible against the murky sky of evening. You could see little else besides the shadowy hugeness and the dim blue glow of the pressor beam lamps which supported it above the surface of the planet. Kirin thumbed his wristlet.

"How did you get here? Was it you that knocked down those patrol craft?"

A familiar mechanical voice answered from the phone strapped to his wrist.

"I became aware 10.2 minutes ago that the force field holding my circuits under control had gone dead.

According to Prime Directive gamma-2, I took to the air, searching out your whereabouts on my own initiative. Then I heard your call and traced your beam. I observed you were being pursued by a squadron of aerial automata, so I intervened with my secondary disruptor banks and destroyed them before they could—"

"All right, all right," Kirin growled. "We get the idea. I'm coming up to your level. Hold your present position and be ready to open the forward starboard lock when I come alongside."

He clicked off and swung the sled up to the seven thousand foot level, ascending until he was even with the slim cruiser. Then he gently nursed the sled alongside with tiny bursts of power. The lock swung back and the lighted interior of the ship glowed in the surrounding darkness.

He helped Caola aboard. The sled swayed a bit in the high winds that blew in frequent gusts at this height above the city, but the danger was minimal. Then, fat, puffing old Temujin heaved his bulk through the circular port and vanished within. Kirin set the controls for a dive and jumped.

The steel grill of the lock bay slammed against the soles of his feet. He looked out to see the sled veer away to the north and vanish in the darkness.

"All right, ship. Seal up and hit a course for Pelizon," he said. The ship silently obeyed.

They were, all of them, exhausted from the strain of the past few hours, tired, battered and hungry. But they were safe and back on the right road again...

We've got nothing to worry about now, except a planet-full of kill-crazy Death Dwarves, Kirin thought sourly.

CHAPTER 12

DARK JOURNEY

The dim ochre globe of Zangrimar shrank beneath their pounding jets and swung away, dwindling and revolving into the black abyss that lies between the stars. The planet of the Witch Queen faded behind them and was lost amidst the darkness.

The ship tested its circuits and reported quietly that it had suffered no damage from the force trap that had intercepted its course and drawn it deep into the Dragon Stars. The temporary usurpation of the control circuits had caused no permanent impairment to its efficiency.

It lifted out of the ecliptic and transposed into that mathematical paradox called the Interplenum, an artificial sub-continuum where the laws governing matter and energy were somewhat different from those observed in normal space. In this weird and technically non-existent region of space, light-speed was no longer the limiting velocity, and interstellar travel was made possible by a slight revision in Einsteinian theory. The flight from Zangrimar to Pelizon would take several hours at normal cruising speeds.

Which was just as well. Kirin had no desire to speed the trip. He was worn out, physically and mentally, and looked forward to some rest before tackling the problem of the Iron Tower and the theft of the Medusa.

They were all worn out, and some rest and refreshment would do them good. Therefore, leaving the problems of navigation in the capable hands (so to speak) of the ship's brain, they showered leisurely, letting the hissing jets of hot, sudsy water steam out the aches and pains from weary muscles. Then followed a hearty lunch; the ship was a prodigal host and the table was laden with delicacies from the vacuum-preserved stores kept aft. Sizzling buphodon steaks in green Fangalonian mushrooms and wine sauce, plenty of steaming vegetables, a succulent fresh salad, and pots of hot black kaff.

Then while fat old Temujin snored lustily in his bunk and Caola curled up to enjoy a sound sleep in the other, Kirin stretched out in the capacious pneumo and napped himself.

* * * *

In sleep he again dipped below the surface of his mind into what was to become a strange new world.

Kirin was no fool. He had twice displayed astounding mind powers unknown to his experience. Something was oddly wrong, and he more than halfway guessed it was the result of the brutal probing he had suffered under the hands of the Nexian Mind Wizard.

As he drifted down through the borders of sleep, he puzzled over the strange experiences. He knew something of the human mind and its mysteries. He had heard that man actually uses only a minute fraction of his brain. The mind is a tenuous web of memory-sequences which are little more than stored electrical impulses. But the brain is a fatty organ made up of nerves and cells. It operates like a chemical battery, generating and storing the electrical impulses of thought. Certain portions of the organ have known uses, they operate as nerve-centers, governing the various life support systems of the body. But vast areas of the brain have no purpose. No known purpose, that is.

For many thousands of years, scientists studying the mysterious phenomenon called thought have postulated and speculated as to the reasons why the human brain contains so many seemingly superfluous nerve-cells. Some authorities argued that the answer might lie in the distant past, that ancient man might have had other or extra senses than those used by modern man. "Lost" senses and abilities, like psychokinesis, the power of mind to manipulate matter; or telepathy, the power of direct mind-to-mind communication; or teleportation, the ability to transport objects or persons across vast gulfs of space without physical motive power.

These curious "wild talents" still occasionally crop up in modern man, although they are exceedingly rare. Hence it was argued that perhaps at some remote era in the distant past all men had these powers. In order to possess these mental abilities, men would need nerve-centers in the brain to govern them, just as he possessed nerve-centers which governed his more mundane senses such as sight, hearing, balance, and so on. Although the wild talents may have died out, the extraneous brain-matter might be explained as vestigial nerve-centers, physical remainders of long-dead powers. For the average human body does contain certain vestigial organs no longer used, such as the vermiform appendix. The organ tends to outlive the use thereof, one ancient sage put it succinctly, as is the way with sages.

So much for the theories of science. But occultism had another explanation. Life memories are recorded in the nerve-cells. Perhaps a man passes on a miniaturized recording of his life memory to his offspring, a cumulative or "racial memory" stored in the so-called unused portions of the brain.

But now Kirin was no longer musing over this and other mental mysteries. He was sound asleep. And in his sleep the truth of the occult theory was shown to him.

For with that sleep, there came a dream.

* * * *

It seemed to Kirin that in his dream he descended deep into himself. He penetrated, by curious and shadowy pathways, that inner citadel called the Unconscious Mind. Here lies the deep sediment of thought, memories long since forgotten by the upper, conscious levels of his mentality. Memories of earliest childhood, of babyhood, even vague blurred impulses recorded while he was still in the womb of his mother.

He passed yet further, through veils of darkness. Now swift visions flickered around him, glimpses of scenes and faces, audible and sensory memories. They passed too swiftly for him to more than glimpse their shape and motion.

These were the recorded life memories of his father and his mother, on an old earth far away.

He voyaged on, ever deeper.

He passed through the memories of many lives, hundreds of lives. The lives of his direct ancestors, life upon life, generation upon generation, century after century, like microfilm recordings.

Thousands of lives flashed by him. He caught only swift flickering glimpses as the small floating brilliant point of utter light that was the "I" of him intersected memory-sequences...

A towering mushroom cloud of incandescent orange and scarlet climbed like an angry giant above the island of Manhattan, stamping it flat with feet of thunder. A memory of the fiery holocaust called the Thirty-Six Minute War...

The dark flashing shapes of MIGs hurtled over Chong-ho-dong Valley... a scrap of memory from a distant ancestor who had fought in the Korean War...

A sleepy French village slumbered on a spring morning. Chickens clucked and squabbled in the dust of a roadway. Beyond the row of beech trees to the east, the deep-throated thunder of big guns grumbled. The tired, tattered legions of the Kaiser, grimly plodding on towards Paris...

The roar of cannon and the drumming of hooves. Steel sabres flashed in a hot dusty afternoon sun. Behind the bellowing cannon, stolid Russian peasant faces stared in amazement at the cavalrymen as they flew straight into the blaze of the cannon. Red-faced, choleric, shouting, Lord Cardigan led the Light Brigade into the jaws of death...

Now the pace quickened. Faster flew the visions...

The skies above London were crimson. Lines of bent backs crept out of the city over the bridges, bearing hastily-assembled belongings. King Charles and the entire court had left that morning. The Great Fire raged on unchecked...

Wind whipped the painted wooden sign to and fro, creaking and squealing. Rain sleeted against the diamond-paned windows of the old, low-roofed inn. But within the Mermaid, fire roared on the grate and painted huge black shadows across the walls and the nodding, smiling bearded men in throat-ruffs and rain-daubed cloaks who sat listening to Ben Jonson talk. In a distant comer, pale young Edmund Spenser called for mulled ale and bent to scan the verses he had just scribbled...

Swifter—and swifter yet! Like great wings beating on the wind, alternately dark and bright...

A dim rainy morning. Knights in mud-splashed cloaks and rust-smeared mail. Their faces were pale and tense beneath shaggy beards and layers of dirt. Awe and terror was in their eyes and their mouths shaped hoarse oaths as they bent humbly beside the great red-golden lion of a man who lay dead with an arrow hideously protruding from one eye. Harold Godwinson was dead... the Saxon cause was lost forever... and William the Norman would be king. They wept beside the fallen champion, kneeling in the mud...

Howling like madmen, their scrawny bare bodies smeared with blue paint, the Picts swept up against the great wall and came scrambling up in the very teeth of the Roman swords. Lucius Albionus cursed thickly and roared an order. Bugles rang cold and clear and reinforcements sprinted along the wet clay roadway. The battle would be long and fierce, but it would end eventually, the tired old Roman thought. But what's the use? Hadrian's Wall will fall in time; even the Empire will fall... why fight and die here in the misty wastes of barbaric Caledonia?...

The flash of a golden helmet in the morning light! Red-cloaked legions swung clanking in tight formation to meet the charge of the bearded savages. Atop his black mare, the Lord Scipio Africanus smiled coldly. He was well pleased. The host of the Carthaginians was crushed; all they had left was the native savages to hurl against the iron strength of Invincible Rome. Soon the glittering African metropolis would fall, and young Rome would triumph, her greatest foe destroyed. The road to Empire lay clear before her... naught could hold her from dominion over the earth...

Night lay, black wings folded, over the frowning zig-gurats of ancient Babylon. All slept, the conquered Persians and their bold Macedonian conquerors, sated with the victory feast. But a light burned in the palace window, where a young man scarce more than a boy bent over ancient documents murmuring archivists set before him. He took a swallow of red wine and bent forward again, holding the parchment map closer to the oil lamp whose wavering glow blazed on his golden hair. Ayé, this was the route to the Indus . . . and when the proud Gangarids had knelt before him... on to fabulous Cathay and the very ends of the earth itself... then, surely, Zeus his father would give him a place among the undying Gods, for he had outdone every man who had ever lived... the fires flickered low, but he saw it not. For flesh is weak and the young grow weary swiftly. And young Alexander slept, exhausted, dreaming of bright glory, unaware, as all men are unaware, that he was doomed... Swift now, almost beyond thought, thousands of lives passing in the flicker of an instant...

They bore him in secrecy out of the mud-brick palace and down the reed-bordered river to the secret tomb where all was ready. The rows of little dark men with shaven heads and linen kilts bowed before him as he passed, as a field of grain bows before the wind. Their voices were lifted as one voice as they intoned the quiet, blessed words:

"May he repose in the Western Mountain, and come forth on the earth to see the disc of the Sun, and may the roads be open to the perfect Spirit which is in the Netherworld! May it be granted to him to walk out, to enter and go forth as a living soul, to give offerings to He-who-is-in-the-Other-World, and to present all good things to

Rê-Horus, to Nekhebt, Lady of Heaven, to Hathor, princess of the Desert, to Osiris, the Great God, to Anubis, Lord of the Sacred Land, that they may grant to him the breathing of the sweet breezes of the North Wind."

And thus the mummy of Narmer the Lion, he who had first united the Upper and the Lower Lands with the strength of his sword, passed into the hidden tomb. The first Pharaoh of Egypt passed through the shadows into the sunlight of the Gods…

* * * *

And he came at length into a shining Presence amidst the gloom of the most ancient of memories. Like a shadow of burning gold It hovered against the darkness.

When the voice spoke, it was low and soft as a whisper, But there was strength in it, and unconquerable youth, and a bright vigor that ages of shadow had not dimmed.

"I am Valkyr," It spake to him softly. "The Lords of Life and Death banished me from Eternity into Time, for that crime of which you will have heard ere now. Thus have I lived through ten thousand million lives, passing from world to world; thus shall I go on forever through innumerable incarnations until I have accomplished the task set for me. Through you, O Kirin, shall I expiate mine ancient sin…"

Here, in the dim shadows of the inmost mind, amongst the shards and tatters of forgotten lives, drowned in the depths of this strange and timeless dream, there could be no amazement. Kirin felt, instead, a boundless wonder. For all his days, he had been host to a God! How strange the thought, and yet, in a way, how very fitting. For was not he, too, a thief?

"I have long since grown weary of the stale monotonies of mortal life," the Voice went on softly. "Life after life offered, but repetition of the same narrow range of emotions, the same few small senses, the same limitations. A human body is but a sordid prison to one of the Immortals, O Kirin. Hence I submerged myself deep within the mind of my hosts, dreaming of past glory… and of glory to come."

Did the dim flames beat higher for a moment? Did traces of bygone splendors blaze up within the ghost of the banished divinity? Kirin could not be sure.

"Soon we shall enter the Tower, you and I. I can help you but little, for my strength has ebbed over the aeons of my imprisonment, and I am weary from loss of the strength I have already given unto you, although I grudged it not. Be wary then, O Kirin, and step with care, for I can help you but once more before the end…"

A strange conflict rose within his dreamself. How to explain to that gentle, sorrowful, weary being that he did not want to give up the Medusa to another! How display before that crippled angel who slept within him, the shame of his own greed? Even as he struggled to find the right words, he felt the dream ending, and fought against it…

* * * *

He became conscious that a hand was shaking his shoulder and he opened his eyes to see old Temujin peering down with a smile and to hear him say:

"Wake up, lad. We're here! Pelizon is in the scopes."

CHAPTER 13

ZARLAK STRIKES

In a dark cavernous room far underground, lit by the cold flare of permabulbs, a gaunt man sat alone at a huge table of dark wood.

He was robed in dark glittering stuff. Black silks rustled crisply to every motion as he turned the leaves of the ancient book that lay before him on the table. Sequins of jewelled light winked and flashed as he turned the pages; they were sewn along the folds of the voluminous robes that cloaked him from men's eyes.

His face was an oval of darkness beneath the enshadowing cowl of his robe. Only his eyes could be seen. They were grey and cold as ice, but fierce as flame. As he hovered immobile over a rune-scrawled page of the old manuscript book, only his eyes seemed to live. They burned and seethed with restless energy. A cold, subhuman cruelty was in their icy glare, and the hot banked fires of unholy and unscrupulous ambition.

The book over which the robed and masked figure bent so intently was old. A thousand centuries has passed since alien hands had inscribed those sheets of wrinkled yellowing leather with uncouth hieroglyphics. The book that lay before him on the mighty table was older than recorded human history. The river clay whereof men were someday to fashion bricks wherewith to raise the walls of Ur of the Chaldees was still fresh and wet when these crumbling pages were inscribed. The stones of Cheop's pyramid still slept amid unbroken hills along the Valley of the Nile. The titanic glittering wall of ice that came grinding down across the world out of the ultimate and boreal north had but recently withdrawn into its fastnesses. Man was young, scarce more than a beast that had learned to stand erect and toy with tools. An aura of almost palpable age hung about the old book; it was impregnated with the dust of a hundred thousand years of slow time.

Whatever the veiled man had hoped to find in the ancient codex eluded him. With a bitter curse he closed the book and shoved it from him, and sat back in his great throne-like chair, brooding, eyes of cold fury inscrutable as they stared hungrily into the cavernous gloom of the subterranean chamber.

A sound behind him. The clink of steel on steel. A dark curtain was drawn to one side by a gnarled and claw-like hand. The black mouth of a tunnel was thus exposed, behind the hangings. From the entrance came forth into view a small, dwarfed figure clad in weird armor of steel. Fantastical in design, the armor was scrawled over with writhing dragons and snarling devil-heads. The dwarf was clad entirely in steel, save for his gnarled and twisted hands and his sallow, frog-like face.

He was incredibly ugly. His mouth was a broad lip-less gash and his three eyes were glowing slits filled with evil malignant glitter. His skull-like head was devoid of hirsute adornment.

"Master!" he croaked. The robed figure turned to regard him.

"Speak!" the robed one commanded harshly.

"We have lost contact with Pangoy," the Death Dwarf said. "His receptors went dead in the third quarter of the Hour of the Toad."

"Death, or unconsciousness?" the Veiled One demanded.

"Death."

The word echoed in the silence, fading away into dim whispers. The robed man with the black-masked face regarded the dwarf steadily, with eyes of cold grey flame. Zarlak, the Master of the Death Dwarves and Lord of Pelizon was filled with the bitterness of failure. The age-old book he had searched through fruitlessly and had just shaved aside had been his last hope. Ever since coming to this wilderness world, the Veiled One had striven for one purpose: to find the secret of the Iron Tower. He had searched the crumbling archives of the death cult, but in vain. Old rumors and whispers he had tracked down, but for naught. Now he sought in the ancient Books of Power for the key that would unlock the charmed and demon-guarded gates of the Iron Tower, and the Books had failed him.

The failure of his connection with Pangoy on Zangrimar was yet another disappointment. His mask hid the expression of rage and frustrate fury that writhed and snarled across his face. But his eyes blazed with unholy wrath and cruelty. The Dwarf was forced to turn his eyes away with a little shudder; the flaming fury in Zarlak's gaze was beyond his endurance.

"Give me the tapes!" Zarlak said. Silently, the Dwarf handed his master a tangle of grey plastic ribbon, whereon black wavering lines were drawn. Zarlak slid them through his black-gloved fingers, studying them.

"The last recordings show that he surprised a slave girl in his quarters. As he was questioning her, the Earthling awoke and they fought. The Earthling, Kirin, seems to have slain Pangoy…"

"I can read the telemetry, fool," Zarlak grated. He threw the tapes from him with a soundless snarl. Pangoy had been invaluable. The Nexian had never known that telepathic receptors had been surgically implanted in his brain-tissue before he had ever reached the planet Zangrimar. The Mind Wizard never knew he was an involuntary spy for Zarlak, Lord of Pelizon. Now his involuntary servitude was ended, and still Zarlak did not have the secret of the Iron Tower.

The Dwarf, Vulkaar, edged nearer.

"What now, Lord?" he whispered. The cold glare of Zarlak brooded on the gloom.

"Now the Earthling will come here, of course," he said. "If he is able to escape the clutches of the Witch Queen alive, and gain his ship."

"Will he be able to do so? The Witch is powerful..." the Dwarf, Vulkaar, said dubiously.

"So was Pangoy," said Zarlak. "His mastery of the mental forces was extraordinary—which is why the Mind Wizards of Nex dispatched him to Zangrimar in the first place. Only one with his power could destroy Azeera before she plunged half a galaxy in war." An invisible smile crawled across the masked lips of Zarlak. "The fool succumbed to her wiles despite his powers. He fell hopelessly in love with the Witch Queen... and she accepted him into her service, knowing what a weapon his mental powers would be. She never knew, nor did he, that his own brain broadcast to my receptors everything he saw or heard."

Vulkaar cackled a peal of gloating laughter.

"That love was your doing, Master!"

"Yes." Zarlak smiled. "It was a master-stroke. I was a novice in the Mind Schools of Nex in those days... when I learned Pangoy had been selected for the mission, I lured him to my cell and implanted the telepathic receptors within his brain. And hypnotized him so that he would lust for the Witch and fall under her spell. I took a chance, hoping that Azeera was still enough of a woman to be flattered by his adoration and accept his service, rather than having him slain. All went well, but now the Earthling has somehow overcome even a Mind Wizard…"

"Then you think this Kirin will escape from Zangrimar?" Vulkaar asked. The Master nodded.

"If he was strong enough to destroy the Nexian, he has a chance of eluding the grasp of the Witch Queen. And if he does, he will doubtless come to Pelizon."

The sallow Dwarf in the fantastic steel armor mused thoughtfully on this. The Death Dwarves of Pelizon guarded the Iron Tower with an age-old fanaticism; no intruder could be permitted into the Tower; all were slain. But the Veiled One had lured Vulkaar from his vows and won his obedience. The Dwarf's heart was a blazing crucible of greed and lust; by playing subtly on his greed, Zarlak had bound him to his service and shared the secret of his intentions with him. Vulkaar proved a precious ally. Together they were consumed with but a single wish: to rape the Iron Tower of its sacred treasure, the Medusa, and with the power of the Demon's Heart, to gain mastery of many worlds. Vulkaar slavered at the thought: the Master had promised him gold… and women… Earthling women!

"What shall we do if he comes here, Master?"

"We shall lay a little trap and catch him in our snare," the Lord of Pelizon replied.

"Before he reaches the Tower?"

The master laughed. His voice dropped to a soft, silken purr:

"No, you fool. After he has stolen the Medusa and is leaving the Tower!"

The cunning in his voice delighted Vulkaar. The little Death Dwarf capered and leaped about the gloom-shrouded chamber, crowing with glee. And the harsh laughter of the Veiled One rose to fill the darkness of the stone room with ringing peals of demoniac mirth…

* * * *

"I don't like this, lad. I don't like it one bit!" old Temujin puffed, toiling along behind Kirin and the girl. The grey cindery plain was rough underfoot, and the old Magician's sandals kept sinking into the harsh crystals. Above the sky was dark and empty, filled with drifting vapors.

Kirin didn't like it either. It was odd. He had been told the Death Dwarves guarded the lands about the Iron Tower with great care and cunning. Where, then, were they?

Kirin and his companions had broken out of the Interplenum in a distant orbit around the parent star of Pelizon world. They crept into the system with stealth, their ship carefully shielded against detection. The planet Pelizon lay beneath their keel, a dull grey sphere of wrinkled stone, whose barren shores were washed by dark and nameless seas. The daylight terminator cut across the bleak plateaus as they drifted down towards it on tiny bursts of power from the steering jets.

No patrols. No planet-based radar stations. Nothing.

It was more than strange, it was alarming.

They landed with great secrecy on the night side. Still no alarms. Stratosphere reconnaissance showed no campfires, no tribal towns, no gatherings. The Iron Tower was alone and unguarded on its bleak stony plateau under the mist-robed skies. Curious…

Warily they disembarked, to gain the base of the Tower on foot. Either their stealth and secrecy had eluded the attention of the Death Dwarves, or the Tower was not kept under as strict and close a system of surveillance as they had supposed…

Caola stifled a gasp and clutched Kirin's arm, pointing wordlessly.

At that moment, the skies cleared.

The curtain of vapor was torn aside by cold winds. The icy glitter of the stars blazed down, and the lambent glory of the moons, bathing the barren stone in ashen light.

Ahead, the Iron Tower thrust against the naked heavens.

Kirin sucked in his breath and chewed on his lip, studying the fantastic structure intently.

It was not as tall as he had expected. The Earthling was not exactly sure what he had expected: some splendid, spidery, incredibly tall structure, perhaps. But he had been wrong.

The Tower was a ziggurat, a step-pyramid, built in nine levels. Low and squat and solid, it loomed ahead of them like a man-made mountain, thrusting up out of the severe flatness of the rocky plateau.

It was a grim, prison-like structure. It looked like a fortress, all harsh angles and blocky corners. In the pallid wash of moonfire that lay upon it, the Tower did not look as if it were sheathed in iron. It had not the gloss, the gleam, of metal. Instead it was raised from some porous, lava-like stone, grey and dense and rough-surfaced.

It lifted above the plain, level upon level, ascending into the night. Somehow it looked ominous. Sinister. A weird aura of menace clung about the ziggurat. It radiated a clammy feeling of fear!

They stood, the three of them, staring up at the thing that squatted there amidst the barren plain. There was an atmosphere of alienage about the stone building—something they could not explain. But it was somehow obvious that no human hands had built that looming structure, although none of them could have put into words exactly why they felt thus.

They stared at the Tower. Kirin with a narrowed, measuring gaze, his mouth twisted into an ironic half-smile; Caola, who clung to his arm, lifted her pale face to the Tower, and her features were haunted with a shadow of foreboding and fear; and as for the doctor, he goggled at it with open mouth.

"I say again, lad, I don't like this—it's too quiet, I smell a trap!" he hissed.

Kirin shrugged off the emotion of dread and awe that had fallen upon him since his first sight of the Tower.

"Forget it. Come on—and keep your eyes open, both of you!"

They continued forward. From time to time, Kirin glanced in a puzzled fashion at his left wrist. There a leather band was strapped to his arm. Dials glowed phosphorescently.

The miniature detector was very simple: it was heat-sensitive along a monodirectional beam, and delicate enough to register any warm-blooded lifeform larger than a cat. From time to time he swept the surrounding plain with the beam: it registered nothing. The Tower was unguarded.

Unguarded by living things, at least.

They plodded on. The nearer they came to the Tower, the vaster it became. At first sight it had seemed of no particular consequence, a low, squat structure like a citadel or a tomb. Now, as they drew nearer, the true size and proportions of the Tower dawned on them. It was colossal. The longer they moved towards it, the larger it seemed. At last, after almost an hour, they stood before the base of it, and could see the fortress in true perspective.

It was somewhat more than half a mile long, and almost half a mile high. It was the largest single building Kirin had ever seen or heard of; even the central citadel of Azeera's city back on Zangrimar would have been dwarfed beside it, and that was not one building, but many linked together.

Truly, only a god could have built this thing, he thought, staring up at it.

The ultimate marvel was that it was not built in blocks of stone: it was all of one piece! As for the grey, rough, porous rock whereof it was fashioned, Kirin had never seen such stone before. He ran his palm over it. It seemed as dense and tough as metal. All of his strength could not dislodge a crumb of the rough surface.

It seemed to the eye to be fire-blasted. Terrific flames had poured over it once, aeons ago. The surface was roiled and pocked, like slag, like volcanic lava.

Had the god molded it all at once out of liquid stone?

A portal yawned blackly before them.

There were no guards. No alarm posts or signal-rays. Again he swept the area with his heat-detector. Nothing. It made him feel tense and wary. Something was wrong. Something was very wrong. There should have been guards...

"I'm going in," he grunted.

The girl caught his arm. "Do you think you should?"

"Sure. I've committed the charts to memory. I know every foot of the passage. And I'd better get going now, before the Death Dwarves show up. We seem to have caught them on their night off!" His lips twisted in a faint grin at the sickly jest. He did not feel very humorous, standing there at the black mouth of the passage, in the very shadow of the inhuman stone thing that was half as old as the Universe itself. In fact, he felt scared, but he throttled it down, crushed it. And he knew that the longer he stood here, the worse it would get. Better get inside now while he still had some nerve left.

Temujin plucked at his cloak.

"Lad... lad! Let's forget it... to Chaos with the Medusa, and to Chaos with the high and holy plans of Trevelon! Let's get away from here, while we've still got a whole skin and a sane mind, the three of us! Let's get off this cursed world of shadows and brooding menace."

He shook his head.

"No, Doc—though you tempt me, no, I'm going to do it. At least, I'm going to try it. No thief in history ever succeeded in stealing the Medusa. Maybe I can break that record..."

And he turned on his heel and went into the Iron Tower. He did not look back at them. In an instant the darkness had swallowed him.

"Do you think he will do it?" Caola asked. The old Magician shrugged.

"The Gods know, lass. But if anybody can, Kirin's the lad to do the job," he said, heaving a heavy sigh.

"And what are we supposed to do—just wait here for him to come out again?" the girl asked, casting an anxious look about her at the grim landscape, the moon-washed mountain of stone, and the gloomy sky wherein stars burned with a far icy glitter. She shivered. "I don't like it; I feel... as if someone is watching me!"

Old Temujin patted her hand. "Nonsense, lass! Relax; don't worry. The lad will be all right, I promise you. And there is nothing for us to do but wait. The Gods only know how long it will take Kirin to make his way through the depths of that accursed Tower to the treasure-chamber. We must be patient and wait for his return."

A cold, mocking voice spoke from behind them.

"We shall wait for him together," said Zarlak. Then, to the Death Dwarves who companioned him: "Seize them!"

CHAPTER 14

MAGIC MAZE

Kirin went forward in utter darkness. The passage ran straight for a time, deep into the god-made mountain of iron-hard stone. The portal through which he had come dwindled behind him, a dim rectangle of faint light. Then the passage took a sharp turn to the right, and the distant gateway vanished. He went forward into unbroken gloom.

Now that he was actually within the Iron Tower, his dread and awe vanished. He felt fully alert, poised, cool. Every sense was honed to razor-sharpness. His nerves were steady, his pulse-beat was calm. He felt keyed up to maximum power; totally in command of himself and ready for anything.

From his belt-pouch he drew forth a curious device which he strapped to his brow. From brackets attached to the strap two black discs snapped down in front of his eyes. Protruding from the strap in the center of his forehead was a metal tube. From this a pulsating beam of force throbbed. It bathed space in front of him, and when the pulsations of force encountered a solid barrier, then they reflected back. The black discs in front of his eyes were rendered sensitive to the force beam. They pictured a three-dimensional image of the obstacles in front of him. It was like a 3D version of radar.

He could have used a simple light-beam: others in the past who had ventured within the tomb-like Tower may have used lights. That would account for the dry and brittle bones that crunched under his feet.

Above him, in niches along the walls of the passage, silver birds with cruel hooked beaks sat motionless. Life had been infused into eternal metal. But they slept: only visible light would awaken the rapacious robot birds, sending them forth to rend and slay. They did not react to the invisible pulsations of the force-probe. Which is why he wore the headdress mechanism instead of simply carrying a torch or light-tube.

Now he came to the first of the obstacles. Huge swinging blades, like meat-cleavers, swung down from the roof, and up from grooves in the floor, and out of the walls. They went snickering past, slashing at empty air in an eternal dance of death. He stood observing them, remembering the data given in the documents from Trevelon, memorizing the rhythm of their strokes. Then he sprang amidst the blades as they went hissing past. He maneuvered between them and through them, but it was chancy in the extreme. The force-probe was an alternative to sight, but not really a substitute. Half blinded, he moved among the flying knives. The sweat sprang out over his forehead. It trickled down his sides under his tunic. His inner thighs were clammy with perspiration.

Then he was through the area of the invisible scythes and he stood on safe ground once again. For a time he simply stood there until he stopped trembling; stood there breathing deeply, feeling the tension drain out of him like water draining from a squeezed sponge, recovering his self-control. He had passed the phototropic birds and the flying knives safely, but even deadlier traps lay before him.

When his self-control was complete, he went forward again, but slowly, cautiously, counting the footsteps.

Finally he came to an area of flat stone. He inched forward with extreme caution, slipping a harness from his pouch. He strapped curious gloves and bootlets to his hands and feet. Cups of tough plastic were fastened to the palms of the gloves and to the toes of the bootlets. He thrust his palms against the left wall of the passage, high up. The suction cups adhered. He levered himself up above the floor and stuck the toe-cups against the wall. Then, slowly and painfully, he inched his way along the wall of the passage, level with but a couple of feet above the floor.

For the floor here was an illusion. It was not solid rock, although it resembled it. It would have borne his weight for a few yards: thereafter it became a deadly quasi-solid state of matter like quicksand. It would have sucked him down greedily to a horrible death.

He moved across the face of the wall like a human fly.

It was slow going. In no time at all, the muscles of his arms and shoulders and thighs began to ache abominably. He gritted his teeth and struggled on.

After an eternity he passed the area of the liquid stone and was able to come down to the solid floor again. He felt exhausted. But he could not rest yet. Greater tasks lay ahead of him and he must press on before his strength failed.

He came to a region where the floor was covered with a raised design. Eight inches tall, a wandering maze of narrow stonework scrawled over the flooring. The edges of this miniature maze were sharp as razors and hard as diamond.

He must go forward, threading through the maze, avoiding contact with the knife-like edges. Even the tough plastic of his boots could not protect him from the savage keenness of the blade-edged maze. Nor could he continue using the suction harness on the walls, unless he were a superman. For the knife-maze extended for three hundred yards and his muscles could not endure the torment of wall-walking for such a distance.

But the maze could be traversed, and safely, if one kept cool and kept one's nerve. To do it in utter darkness was agony. But he inched his way forward slowly, step by step, using the force-probe to read the ground ahead of him, holding in his mind a clear picture of the one safe route through the maze. He could do it. He knew he could do it. And he did.

It took two hours of excruciating effort and patience. But he came through it safely, although his nerves were frayed clear to the bone.

He rested for a time, and took nourishment from the concentrated rations he carried with him, washed down with a healthy draught of strong brandy.

Then, when he felt rested and restored, he went forward again into the blackness deep within the heart of the Iron Tower…

* * * *

Seven more tests he passed, each more difficult and ingenious than the last. Some of them took every ounce of strength and limberness in his body; others demanded a clear head and a steady nerve. He only managed to endure the torment because he knew what was coming and how to surmount it. It would have been impossible to penetrate the maze safely not knowing the way.

There was a forest of howling pillars through which he wove a narrow and perilous path. Carven mouths roared at him and empty black eye-pits glared with inanimate hate…

There was a knife-thin bridge that arched across a chasm of living flames whose curling tendrils clutched and lashed at his limbs...

There was a bottomless pit whereover he must cross by an Invisible bridge that was as slick as glass. Great winds rose in this pit out of the center of the world and strove to thrust him off balance...

There was a resonant echo-chamber hung with dangling spears of stone where the slightest sound reverberated deafeningly and the stone spears could be dislodged by the slightest whisper...

Through these and other perils he passed by the use of caution and patience and strength and grim nerve... aided, it must be confessed, by certain clever devices he bore with him against the hour of need. Fore-warned is fore-armed, and the grey philosophers of Trevelon had searched well through their magic skills.

In a safe place he rested and even slept for a time, napping huddled in his cloak against the shelter of the wall. He must husband every atom of strength against further need. And when he awoke, he went forward again.

* * * *

No man had ever come this far before. At least, there were no bones here.

He felt very alone. The god still slept within him. He could have used a few miracles, he thought with a grim, weary smile. He felt as if he had come many miles by now. And, for all he knew, perhaps he had—despite the known dimensions of the Tower.

Space and time were distorted here, twisted into new contours by the spell of the god. He felt so weary, he wondered if he had been in the maze hours... or days?

He went on.

He was past the greater number of the death-traps now. He had passed the corridor of stone gladiators where living statues, their arms honed to stone swords, listened alertly for the slightest sound, ready to kill. He had traversed the fiery corridor where jets of flame lashed erratically at any passing shadow. He had survived the chamber of ice where blasts of freezing cold congealed any warm-blooded thing that ventured therein. His supply of protective devices was now exhausted.

He would need no more artificial aid, he had been told, from this point on. He hoped the mages of Trevelon know what they were talking about. He went forward warily.

And came at last to the door of the treasure chamber itself. He had come through a thousand perils untouched. And as he stood gazing at the door to the chamber wherein the Heart of Kom Yazoth was kept (so the inscription read), he felt his heart sink within him. For one last peril lay before him. A peril he had not been prepared to face.

He tasted the bitterness of defeat and failure. He growled a despairing curse at the distant philosophers who had not warned him of this…

Between where he stood and the door to the inmost chamber, the floor fell away in a bottomless abyss.

An abyss a hundred yards across!

Kirin groaned and rubbed his brows. He could not fly, he could not jump, and his suction harness had been discarded, together with all surplus weight, far behind him, when he passed over a pit of knives on a slender rope that could bear only his weight alone.

This was the end of the quest. He could neither go back nor go forward.

He was doomed.

* * * *

He slept there on the brink of the abyss. He was utterly exhausted in body and mind; worn out, with a weariness that ran bone-deep.

He awoke to hunger and thirst, but his food supplies had been cast aside together with the no-longer-needed equipment. The mages had warned him, through Temujin, that at the area of the pit of knives he must abandon every bit of extra weight. Once he had reached the Medusa (said they), the return passage would be magically brief and without any perils.

He wished he had retained the suction harness. Although in his exhausted state he greatly doubted he would have been able to span the abyss by clinging with vacuum cups to the walls. Still, he would have had a fighting chance.

This way he had no chance at all.

He searched the edge of the abyss from one wall to the other, testing every inch of empty space along the edge. It was just possible there was an invisible bridge...

But there was none.

He sat on the edge of the abyss, dangling his heels, staring into emptiness.

What happened now?

Well, he could stay here and starve to death. Slowly.

Or he could try to retrace his path, and die under slashing knives or flailing limbs, or the searing lash of fire-jets, or one or another of the dooms he had passed through with the aid of his mechanisms.

Neither was a very attractive prospect.—

Or he could simply leap into the abyss. It looked bottomless, but it was choked with gloom and he could not tell. At any rate, it would be a swift and merciful death, over in moments. Better than a slow, agonizing death by starvation. Better than dying under the torment of a broken back from the stone gladiators, or burning alive in the fire-jets, or freezing in the chamber of cold.

He could not decide what to do. He sat there idly contemplating his doom. He had never been this close to death before. That is, to certain death. Oh, he had flirted with destruction many times in his perilous career. But always he had won through to freedom. This time, his position was hopeless. It was a rather unpleasant thought.

Strangely enough, he found himself thinking of his friends. His death would mean their deaths as well. For the robot ship would not open to admit Temujin or Caola. They would wait beyond the portal of the Tower for his return. But he would never return, and they would eventually be caught and slain by the Death Dwarves.

Nor could he do anything to prevent this! The thought galled him unbearably. His own death was one thing: grim enough, but at least he had gone into this with his eyes open, knowing the risks he took, and confident that he could surmount them. But to have the deaths of the old man and the girl on his conscience as well—that was an ugly burden to carry down into the eternal darkness with him. He cursed wearily, damning the wise men of Trevelon who had foreseen every hazard but this last one, damning the dead god within him who had built this accursed tower of stuff so dense he could not even use his signal bracelet to summon aid from the ship. Seven times he had tried to punch a rescue call through the dense stuff of the Tower and seven times he had failed. Nor would the ship do anything on its own initiative. Its intelligence was, after all, limited. It would sit there on the plain till doomsday, unless attacked. And since it was completely invisible and indetectible, he doubted if the Death Dwarves would attack it.

It was hopeless. Utterly.

What about the god who slept within his deepest mind? Could even Valkyr do anything to get him out of this predicament? He had tried to summon the god, to contact it, to communicate. But he had failed to rouse the ghost of the deity.

His situation was completely hopeless.

Idly, he wondered why the grey ones of Trevelon had not foreseen this last hazard. There must be a reason. They had anticipated everything else. What possible explanation could there be? He tried to think, tried to cudgel his wits into some semblance of their former alert acuteness. But he was too tired, too hungry. And thirst was becoming a torment to him. It seemed like days since he had last had anything to drink.

* * * *

He napped again, falling into a light, fitful, uneasy slumber. He half hoped that in the extremity of his need he would contact the ghost of Valkyr within his ancestral memory, but nothing chanced. After a time he awoke, no longer quite as weary, but hungrier and thirstier than before. He knew he could not endure this for long. Thirst drives men mad long before hunger can kill them. He resolved to spare himself that kind of an end. Far better, a swift leap into the abyss, a fast, clean death in instants, than a lingering agony, giggling with madness, chewing on his own flesh. He would go out like a man, not like some animal thing, raving in the darkness of a mind gone mad.

He looked again at the abyss.

And, all of a sudden, an idea came to him. A mad idea, a wild concept, surely. But there was a dim chance.

He held the notion at arms' length, turning it about, looking at it from every angle. There was just the slimmest chance in the world that it could be the answer…

He looked again at the abyss. For a very long time now, Kirin had gone forward through lighted corridors and chambers. He was long past the darkness that drenched the outer portions of the maze, long past the time he had depended on the force-probe, and had needed the black mirrors before his eyes to "see" his way. The probe equipment, too, had been thrown away when he had lightened his burden of everything superfluous.

Now he wished he had it.

For perhaps… perhaps … the abyss was only an illusion, a distortion of perspective alone. Perhaps it was only a yard across, and the optical laws were themselves twisted and bent to make the yard seem to stretch for a hundred times its actual length. Perhaps.

If it were so, the illusion would only be visible from his particular angle. That is how perspective works. And however the Master Mages of Trevelon had peered into the impenetrable depths of the Tower to map the path he must follow, perhaps they had looked down on the abyss: from that angle, perhaps it seemed only a yard or two wide, hence they had not deemed it worthy of mention, since a man could easily jump across it.

He examined the idea thoughtfully. He did not examine it very long. There was no use in spending time over it.

It was the only chance he had. Slim, but still a chance. And any chance is better than none, he thought grimly. Any chance at all…

He would try to leap across the abyss.

If his guess was correct, he would land safely before the door to the treasure-chamber.

If his guess would was wrong, he would fall to his death in the abyss.

At least it would be a swift death, and a clean one.

So he jumped...

CHAPTER 15

THE TRIUMPH OF VALKYR

Temujin waited a long time before the portal that led into the Iron Tower. Night passed slowly, and at length a dull grey morning dawned over the rim of Pelizon. Still he waited on, feeling neither weariness nor hunger.

After a long time, Kirin emerged into view and stood in the gateway. He was nearly naked, his garments torn away, his body battered and bloody and smeared with dirt. His face was haggard and worn, but his dark eyes gleamed with accomplishment.

Under his arm was a bundle about the size of a human skull. It was wrapped in gorgeous silken stuff of dark glittering purple, but vagrant gleams of light escaped through the folds of the wrappings. It seemed very heavy, from the careful way the Earthling handled it.

Temujin hurried up to where Kirin leaned exhaustedly in the doorway. Kirin regarded him with a wry grin.

"Well, I made it," he said hoarsely. He did not add by the skin of my teeth. Once he had correctly guessed the illusory nature of the abyss before the inmost door, his path was cleared of all obstacles. The door opened at a touch. Within he had found a room of hewn stone, with a rough altar which bore the mighty crystal, cloaked in the sparkling, night-dark silks.

The way back had been straight and simple: an unobstructed passage that led directly to the front portal, avoiding the many twists and turns of the hazardous way in. He felt battered and drained, but triumphant.

He had done what no other being had done since Time began. He had stolen the Heart of Kom Yazoth, and the key to the control of the Universe lay in the bend of his arm.

Temujin came toward him with quick light steps, one hand thrust out.

"Give it to me now. You will be well paid," the fat little Magician said. Through the haze of his exhaustion, Kirin noticed but did not pay mind to the air of strangeness that clung about the doctor. Had he been in full possession of his faculties, he might have wondered at the glaze in Temujin's eye, the lack of expression on his face, the mechanical tone of his voice. But these things he did not notice.

"Uh, sure," he grunted, peering around. "Where's Caola?"

"She is nearby, resting. Let me have the Medusa now."

"Sure. Any sign of Zarlak and his Dwarves?"

"None whatsoever. All has been quiet. I will take the—"

Kirin straightened. His eyes were reluctant.

"Yeah, all right. But here, let's have a look at it. We've been through a lot for this chunk of junk; let's see what we got." He pulled the silks away and held the gem up into the light so Temujin could see it.

It was an oval mass of glittering crystal, dull and cloudy and opaque. Like a thick glass egg. Unfaceted, rough-hewn, and heavy as lead.

Thick, curdled radiance coiled within it. It flashed with small star-like flakes of gemfire. Light shone from it, dimly green and gold. The coiled luminance within stirred sluggishly, and throbbed like a beating heart. Light ebbed from it in slow pulsating waves.

"Pretty enough," Kirin grunted. Then he turned a curious gaze on the Magician.

Temujin had frozen into immobility the instant his eyes had lighted upon the uncovered Medusa. He stood stiffly, un-moving, his face dead, without animation.

"What's wrong with you?" Kirin asked. He had momentarily forgotten that a glimpse of the Medusa paralyzes the will of all who look upon it, save for him who holds it.

"I am... under the will... of Zarlak," Temujin said dully. "But the sight... of the crystal... broke that spell. Now you... are master!"

"What? How did Zarlak—"

Temujin continued in a thick, lifeless voice that sounded like a man trying to speak through lips numbed by novocaine.

"The Veiled One came upon us shortly after you entered the Tower... his Dwarves seized the lass and myself... he worked a spell upon my mind... forcing me to obey his will..."

"What were you supposed to do?" Kirin demanded harshly.

"Wait for you here and... demand the gem of you... when you came out. Then... uncover the jewel and... put you under its spell..."

"But now there has been a change in plans."

The cold, grating voice spoke from somewhere off to his left. Kirin turned and saw that the ground had opened up, revealing a secret underground tunnel with a cunningly-disguised trapdoor. No wonder his heat-detector had not disclosed the hiding-place of the Death Dwarves! They had been underground, waiting in the tunnel, while he only scanned the surface of the ground!

Now Zarlak stood in the tunnel entrance, his face carefully turned away so that he would not come under the awesome power of the crystal. There were a score of the little ugly men with three eyes with him. Their eyes were bandaged in black cloth so that their wills were not seized by the rapture of the Medusa. Kirin saw that they held Caola helpless.

"Well, a clever trick," Kirin grunted sourly. "Too bad it didn't work. I hold the Medusa and you dare not send your men against me. They can't fight blindfolded this way, and if they catch a glimpse of the stone... they become my men, don't they?" He grunted a coarse laugh. "Looks like a checkmate to me, Zarlak."

"Not," Zarlak said suavely, "while I hold your 'queen', Earthling." His voice dropped to a throaty purr. "Cover the gem and set it down and back away, unless you would like to watch while my servant Vulkaar carves his name on the wench's breasts."

Kirin felt a leaden weight gather in his guts. Suddenly he felt very, very tired. It had been a long fight, and it was lost, that was all. Lost. To hell with the Medusa! Let this madman have it from now on: what did he care? All he wanted was something to eat and drink, and a place to lie down and sleep for a while. Let the star worlds look after themselves. Why should he, Kirin of Tellus, star thief, be the guardian of their destinies?

"All right, you win," he heard himself croak in a dull voice. "Let the girl go. You can have the crystal. Here—"

He held it out, offering—

And the god Valkyr woke within him.

He felt a supernatural power surge up through every tingling nerve and cell and tissue of his body. He felt a new level of awareness spring to life within his waking mind. With the last faint vestiges of his waning energies, the god struck out at Kirin's right hand.

Agony seared his nerves! As if his hand was suddenly thrust to the wrist in boiling water!

He snatched his hand back.

And the crystal fell.

And shattered against the paving stone of the doorway.

* * * *

There fell a hush. No one spoke or moved. Kirin gaped at the broken shards of crystal. Temujin, released from the spell of the stone, stared down at its ruin. Zarlak froze, transfigured with fury and despair, his blazing eyes of cold flame riveted on the wreckage of all his plans.

The Heart of Kom Yazoth was broken. Naught remained of it but scattered fragments of bright dust. The curdled, coiling fires within had flickered, and died.

Kirin felt a vast and nameless sorrow well up within him. For a moment he had held the key to the Universe in his hand. Power over a thousand worlds had been in his grasp. He could have been a king, an Emperor, the Overlord of the Galaxy, and he had let the chance slip through his fingers—literally.

A hoarse, terrible cry burst from Zarlak. Kirin turned to stare, and felt a weird sensation—awe, fear and a sort of holy dread. He looked up; they all were looking up.

The heavens rolled aside like a scroll.

The gods stood amidst the stars, staring down at them.

They were vast and awesome, cloudy titanic figures crowned with glory, robed with the thunders.

Their shoulders were like the mountains. Millions of years lay upon them like a cloak.

Their faces were blinding. A man could not look upon them, or meet the brilliance of their supernal gaze.

Rise up, O Valkyr our Brother, for the time of thy punishment is over and done!

And Valkyr rose. A tide of dazzling power passed through Kirin's body and was gone. A presence that had slept within him all his life was gone. He felt a strange sort of inward emptiness, a loneliness beyond words, for the silent, sleeping companion of all his days had departed from him.

A cloud of splendor, Valkyr the Hero of Heaven rose to join his starry brethren.

Long hast thou gone in banishment, deprived of all but a vestige of thy powers, the gods spake. But thou hast now done reparation for thy sins of old; when the mortal, in his weakness, would have surrendered the Heart into the hands of the servants of evil for the saving of the girl, thou didst drain the strength from his fingers, destroying the Heart for ever! Hail unto thee, O Valkyr, thine exile is over. Thy powers and potencies are given unto thee again, and thou art made welcome among the ranks of the Eternals...

And Valkyr rose and stood amidst the shining giants who were the Lords of Life. Young and strong and fair he was, for all his aeons, and a sword of many lightnings lay against his thigh. His face was a glory like unto the sun itself.

O Elder Brothers, he said, *what of these mortals who have aided my age-long quest? I would reward them for their help...*

And the gods made answer, saying, *They have each already found their reward.*

And Valkyr asked, *And what of this Tower that now lieth empty? It hath no longer any purpose. So let it perish, lest it continue to tempt the greedy into peril.. .*

* * * *

Lightning flashed from the heavens. Thunder grumbled and the ground shook under their feet. The frozen Dwarves staggered off balance.

Kirin shouted: *"Caola! Now!"*

The girl tore loose from the hands of her captors and came running across the stony land towards the Earthling. The ground jumped and shuddered again. She tripped and fell, and Kirin picked her up in his arms.

"Doc!" he yelled. "Let's get out of here."

With old Temujin puffing at his side and the girl huddled in his arms, the Earthling stretched his long legs. They headed away from the Tower.

Breath seared his panting lungs. The rocky soil slapped against the soles of his boots. They ran into the wilderness and the primeval structure shrank behind them. At the crest of the hills they paused to catch their breath. Temujin plucked at his sleeve, pointing behind them.

"Look, lad!" he wheezed.

He turned and looked back.

Lightning flickered in the stormy skies. Tongues of white flame shot from heaven to lick out against the mighty Tower. It shuddered under the impact of the electric fire.

It began to come apart.

There was a grating sound of stone on stone. A black crack zigzagged through the facing wall of the Tower. Earth shuddered like a frightened thing. Fragments of facing crumbled and fell away, pelting against the stony plateau. More cracks shot through the grainy rock surface of the ancient building. It trembled to the rumble of subterranean thunders.

Zarlak still stood rooted with awe and terror and despair with his frightened horde about him. One extended an arm and shrieked something. From where they stood on the crest of the hills, Kirin and his friends could not make out his words, but the meaning was obvious.

As they watched, a tremendous slab of stone broke away from the first tier of the Tower. Its shadow fell over Zarlak and he looked up. A hoarse scream of fear and rage was torn from his lips as the massive slab of dark stone came thundering down to bury him under a hill of rubble.

Slowly, the mighty masses of shattered rock rained down on the trembling plateau. Whirling dust clouds rose, obscuring the wreckage of the Iron Tower. Through the seething dust the baleful flicker of lightning-fire blazed on.

The Tower was fallen. It had withstood the assaults of the slow aeons of time, but before the cleansing fire of the gods it could not stand. No longer would the legend of the Tower beckon to the greed and lust for power in the hearts of men.

The gods, whether they were gods in truth, or merely some extra-dimensional race of super-evolved beings far beyond man in power and wisdom and glory, were gone. The skies were veiled in the darkling wings of storm.

As they staggered across the shuddering plateau, whipped by bitter winds and scourged by gusts of blinding dust, Kirin felt tired and battered, but content.

The quest was done. The Heart was destroyed. Never could it be used by Zarlak or the Witch Queen, who now were dead. Nor would any third power-maddened schemer arise to seek it out, its danger was ended.

Holding the sobbing girl in his arms, Kirin felt a strange warmth and tenderness. He had known many women. But he had never known love… until now.

His hand still ached from the touch of the God. Perhaps the tingling paralysis would pass with time. Or perhaps he would never completely recover the use of the hand. It did not matter. Although a one-handed thief would find things difficult, he cared not. With the wealth that Trevelon had promised him he could purchase a luxurious villa on one of the pleasure-worlds on the borders of Valdamar's Empire. He need never pursue his criminal career further.

Which was just as well, considering. The girl's cheek lay warm and soft against his jaw. Her silken hair was whipped by the wind against his face. The heady perfume of her rose to his nostrils. He grinned.

A married man should find a lawful occupation, he thought, with a smile. They staggered on.

And then the sleek hull of the ship loomed before them, as it sensed their nearness and turned off the invisibility-baffles. The airlock opened, they were safe at last, and the long story was done.